DELILAH'S REVENGE:
There is Nothing More Dangerous
for a Man than a Woman with a Plan

By
S. JAMES GUITARD

Literally Speaking Publishing House
Washington, DC
www.LiterallySpeaking.com

DELILAH'S REVENGE. Copyright © 2006
by S. James Guitard

ISBN 10: 1-929642-16-4
ISBN 13: 978-1-929642-16-8
Published by Literally Speaking Publishing House

Legal Division – Literally Speaking Publishing House
LegalDivision@LiterallySpeaking.com
Literally Speaking Publishing House
2020 Pennsylvania Avenue, NW
Suite 406
Washington, DC 20006

This is a work of fiction. Names, characters, places and incidents, other than those in the Bible, are the products of the author's imagination or are used fictitiously. Any resemblance to actual events, locales, or persons, living or dead, except those that appear in the Bible, are entirely coincidental. The Holy Word of God, which is the Bible, and Jesus Christ is Lord and Savior are eternal truths.

LSPH trade cloth printing 2007. Printed in the U.S.A.

HALLELUJAH

God and God alone
is worthy of all the Praise and the Glory.
Jesus Christ is Lord and Savior.

"Preach the word! Be ready in season and out of season. Convince, rebuke and exhort with all longsuffering and teaching. For time will come when they will not endure sound doctrine, but according to their own desires, because they have itching ears, they will heap upon themselves teachers and they will turn their ears away from the truth, and be turned aside by fables."
2 Timothy 4:2-4

"I have fought the good fight. I have finished the race. I kept the faith."
2 Timothy 4:7

Thank You, Jesus, for Your grace. Thank You, Jesus, for Your mercy. Thank You, Jesus, for teaching me that whether or not I am faced with hurt, heartache or hardship, there is always healing through Your name. No matter what trials, tribulations or troubles that come my way, I must always trust You and Your Word, which is the Holy Bible. At times, my life will definitely be filled with moments of pain, persecution and problems, but I still have joy because I understand the power of prayer and praise. I am able through the blood of Jesus Christ to get better versus bitter when faced with life's adversity. I am unsure what type of burdens tomorrow holds, but I am certain of this: Jesus Christ would not have brought me this far to leave me now.

My prayer is that through *Delilah's Revenge* the saved and the unsaved will come to a better understanding of God's love that appears in His Holy Word, the Bible, and the essence of who God is, was, and will always be. Jesus Christ is the way, the truth and the life.

DEDICATION

This novel is dedicated to my grandmother, Bernice Guitard. Your grandson loves you forever. To Helena, Charles, Shaun, Tiomara. Andre, Lauren, Octavia, Olivia, Thia, and Kiara, I love all of you. May the love, strength, power, peace and joy of God be with you in your life.

Special Acknowledgements

To the entire LSPH family, you are history-making. The best team anyone could imagine. J.M. Branch, you have been helpful in so many ways and capacities. There aren't enough titles or words to express all of what you have done. You are gifted, talented, intelligent, have a big heart and much more. Truly you are a great executive editor and even a greater very friend. Shaun Stevenson, Mychelle Morgan, Maurice Calhoun, your leadership in so many areas has been and remains essential. Thanks for having my back. Azania Brown, your consultation and expertise were instrumental and insightful.

I am extremely blessed and thankful that God in His foresight saw fit to connect such a wonderful and gifted woman as Jill Peddycord to *Delilah's Revenge*. Her drive, determination, patience and commitment to this novel have been unwavering.

Special thanks to Rebecca, Victoria, Deborah, Candace, Rachael, Angela, Tiffany, Laura and Shelly for enduring count-less hours of reading, edits and providing feedback.

Thank you, M&M Calhoun Enterprises and CEO, Maurice Calhoun for your world class technical expertise and support with website development and IT assistance. I have and will always be one of your biggest supporters in business and life. I pray that God continues to take you and your business to new heights.

Every time anyone admires the artistic quality of the book cover, think of Rod Dennis of Colabours, Incorporated. He did an extraordinary job. Once again, thank you, Rod, for your support, creativity and vision. The book cover design receives great reviews wherever I go.

I deeply appreciate all of those who tolerated my endless late night calls requesting that they listen to one more chapter of *Delilah's Revenge*. In particular, I would like to thank all of the men who read the writings and validated them with their lives. Special thanks to all the women who took time out of their busy schedules to read *Delilah's Revenge*. Your feedback has been insightful and provocative. The "love" you have shown for the book touches my heart. I am extremely grateful for all the accolades you have given to a book that had you in mind when I created it.

To all of my all-important readers of every ethnicity, race and geographical location throughout the world, thank you so very much for taking time out to read and recommend my books to family, friends and colleagues. Your support makes a difference. Your feedback is always welcomed and important to me. You can reach me by e-mail me at author@JamesGuitard.com. I look forward to hearing from you. Take care and God Bless.

To all the bookstores, book buyers, book clubs, newspapers and magazines, book websites, distributors and radio and television stations, thank you for your willingness to make available to readers a book that has meant so much to me and to so many others. As an author, I am very cognizant of the importance of your role in the book world and am extremely grateful for all that you have done and continue to do. Thank you. Thank you and Thank you. God Bless.

DELILAH'S REVENGE:
There is Nothing More Dangerous
for a Man than a Woman with a Plan

By
S. JAMES GUITARD

CHAPTER ONE

I couldn't kill her enough times to make me happy, but that didn't stop me from trying. Instead, I stared at her bullet-riddled body and repeated what I had told Evelyn several weeks earlier: "I'm gonna tell you this one time and one time only. If I ever see your number in my husband's caller ID again, I'll kill ya. That's a promise." The affair she'd had with my husband had cost me my marriage, and now it had cost her her life. And to think she says I don't keep my word.

Evelyn should have known better. That no good, two-bit, conniving heifer just didn't know who she was messing with. Crystal Champagne Calloway don't play that. You can't have an affair with my husband, become pregnant with his child, leave text messages saying my man is divorcing me, and then turn around and be the one behind releasing sex photos of me on the web—that I didn't even know existed—causing for my mother to have a heart attack in church, while simultaneously being the unidentified source in the newspaper that has the police falsely charging me with aiding and abetting a money laundering, prostitution and drug cartel, and think you're going to have my kids calling you Mommy while I'm locked up in the penitentiary for the rest of my life. Who you kidding?

All of the psychological warfare—messing with my heart and

head games—had taken its toll. The constant, repeated denials and habitual lies of my husband, Steven Calloway, had resulted in my feeling empty as well as fueled my desire to empty every bullet I could into his lover.

In order for this to work, I needed to stay focused, rub away my tears and place rubbing alcohol on my hands in order to remove any traces of the gunshot residue. With a strong alibi, I could wash away the evidence and the bad memory of the adulteress, Evelyn James.

After all I'd been through today, the constant ringing of my cell phone paled to my deep desire to wring my husband's neck.

"Hello?"

"Yes. Is a Ms. Calloway available?"

"This is Attorney Crystal Calloway. How can I help you?"

"Attorney Calloway, this Robert Vilcano of Vilcano Investigative and Protection Services. Per your request, I am contacting you as soon as we uncovered any additional significant leads concerning your case."

"Go on."

"Well, Attorney Calloway, I have good news to share. Based upon a thorough and exhaustive investigation, we have irrefutable evidence that Evelyn James is not having an affair with your husband as previously suspected."

"You obviously don't know what you're talking about, 'cause I know for a fact that Evelyn is having an affair with my husband. Her husband knows it. I know it. So I don't see why you don't know it."

"If you'll let me continue, Ms. Calloway, I have additional information to share."

"First of all, it's not 'Ms. Calloway.' There's your problem right there. It's Attorney Calloway. So if you can't even get that right, then no wonder you don't know what you're talking about. Matter of fact, tell me if I'm wrong. Didn't I share with you that Evelyn's husband, Rodney James, had seen my husband's car numerous times at his wife's job late at night but didn't know it was my husband's car? Didn't Mr. James confirm to you directly that he had recently tracked down on his own that my husband had been secretly sending bouquets of exotic flowers to his wife from that popular new downtown flower shop? Didn't you tell me that Evelyn was pregnant and that she and my husband were reported to have been seen arguing at an abortion clinic? Didn't I share with you that I had knowledge of unexplained credit card charges for jewelry that I never received from my husband?"

Frustrated and agitated by his incompetence and the fact that Evelyn's dead body was less than ten feet away from me, I shouted into the phone, "All I wanted for you to find out was how long the affair had been going on. That's all. Not if there was an affair, just how long has my husband been lying behind my back."

I could have added that I had followed my husband to a remote hotel on the outskirts of town and waited until he left, softly knocked on the door and put on my best fake you out Spanish I-need-a-green-card-don't-deport-me maid accent and burst through the door to find Evelyn in a sleazy baby doll lingerie and rose petals scattered all across the bed and floor.

"Attorney Calloway, I recognize that the information I have shared comes as a surprise and conflicts with what you have uncovered as well as what we initially shared with you in our investigation, but there is a reasonable explanation for the mix up."

"Mark my words, Robert Vilcano. If you took money from my husband or his firm to cover up his extramarital affair, I promise you, I will sue the living daylights out of you myself."

"Attorney Calloway, if you would just listen for a moment, I could share with you that our investigation has determined that it was your teenage son, Shelton, who has been sleeping with Ms. James. My investigators have learned that it appears that your son's use of your husband's car on various occasions contributed to the mistaken identity. The credit card purchases you referenced earlier were made by Shelton in order to buy expensive gifts and gain Ms. James's attention."

"I don't believe you. You're a liar, and I don't appreciate you making up bald-faced lies about my son in order to cover up for my husband."

"Listen, Ms. Calloway, Attorney Calloway, or whatever you wanna call yourself. I don't take kindly to the accusations you are making about me and my company. You asked us to do a job for you, and we have done it. Evelyn James is pregnant with Shelton Calloway's child, not your husband Steven's. The reason that your husband appeared at the clinic when she was getting a prenatal care checkup was either to convince her not to have an abortion or to convince her to have one. We haven't been able to confirm it one way or another. I am, however, one hundred percent sure that your husband is not the father of the child and has not been having an affair with Ms. James or with anyone, for that matter."

"What about the text messages that I received from Evelyn concerning Steven leaving me? How do you explain that?"

"At this time I can't. I can share with you, however, based upon airline passenger records my staff has uncovered that at least on one occasion when you received a text message from Evelyn it would have been impossible for her to have sent it. Her flight was delayed due to inclement weather and was still in the air when you received the message. That doesn't mean, however, that she didn't send the others, but it does mean that at least one of them is a fake or someone else sent it. I can't confirm this or be able to prove it at this time, but it appears that she may have been telling the truth and none of the messages that you received during the last twenty-four hours were from her. According to what you even shared with me earlier, Ms. James did deny that she knew anything about sending you those messages."

What I needed to say wasn't for Mr. Vilcano to hear, but for me and me only. *Crystal, remaining calm is your number one priority. It appears that a lot of what you've come to believe about your husband Steven and Evelyn, and in many ways still do believe, may be a lie, a misunderstanding or an elaborate plot by someone to set you up. You will need to figure that out quickly. Until then, the 38 snub nose revolver dangling from your hand and shaking uncontrollably is rational and makes sense since the conversation with Mr. Vilcano would shake anyone, and I do mean anyone. Right now, you need to gain strength and power from the fact that although you're shaken, your alibi hasn't been.*

"Robert, I want to express to you my deep appreciation for all of your hard work. You and your agency will be substantially compensated for all of your efforts. I only request your continual confidentiality and highest discretion concerning Calloway family matters. As it relates to my earlier comments, please excuse them. They were not meant to be personal. This is a trying time with all that has been happening with me in the news and my family. Truly you can understand that the information you have uncovered is quite disturbing and shocking, especially since it involves my son and my husband. I know I overreacted and just hope you will accept my apology."

After apologizing profusely to Mr. Vilcano, he accepted more than just my apology, but what mattered most to him—a hefty bonus and revised generous compensation package. There was nothing I could do to bring Evelyn James back to life. Her blood had already started to soak into the carpet. According to Robert Vilcano, I was dead wrong. Unbeknownst to him, Evelyn was just dead.

Determined to use all of my legal training and understanding of police protocol and forensic science in order to avoid being caught, I began dialing the number of the man who will be instrumental in my ability to get away with murder.

In the midst of dialing my brother in-law, DJ, it suddenly hit me. "Oh, my God, I just killed my grandchild."

CHAPTER TWO

With a level of confidence and style that most women would envy, De'Borah Harriston stood at the church sanctuary doors wearing a stylish designer ensemble so sophisticated and eye-catching that a trustee damn near almost dropped the collection plate and his religion trying to get another glance of her revealing low-cut neckline. De'Borah's breasts were more out than some men in the choir. Clearly the older women in the house of worship were quite offended, but it made no difference to De'Borah. It wasn't their attention or approval she was after.

When the choir finished its hymn and the customary shouting of "Hallelujah, Hallelujah," De'Borah gracefully made her presence known throughout the congregation by sashaying down the sanctuary's middle aisle. The usher escorted her to what he thought was an appropriate pew in light of how crowded the church was due to the celebration of the pastor's anniversary.

Despite what should have been apparent, the usher didn't recognize that a woman of Ms. Harriston's stature would never accept sitting so far back on such a special occasion. With a gesture that said, "Follow me. Your input is no longer needed," she brushed off the usher's suggestion and gracefully proceeded to walk to the roped off second row, center pew reserved for dignitaries, directly facing the newly renovated glass pulpit.

Pastor David Josiah Goodwell was just entering the sanctuary wearing a robe that King Solomon would have wanted to borrow. The Reverend Doctor's handsome facial features were perfectly blended into a six-foot-three, two-hundred-and-fifty-pound body frame that looked like it had been chiseled out of Godiva milk chocolate. A quick glance around the congregation let De'Borah know that women throughout Mount Caramel Baptist church were being touched, and this time it wasn't by the Holy Spirit. Pastor Goodwell was driving them all crazy. Like chocolate syrup on top of ice cream on a hot summer day, he was dripping in Power, Strength, Authority and Respect.

Outside of the pulpit, De'Borah's seat location was one of the best in the house, and that is the way Ms. Harriston expected it to be—premium seating for one of the finest women, if not the finest woman, in the church. In every facet of life, De'Borah wanted the best of everything, including the pastor of the fastest growing church in the state, minus his wife, of course.

CHAPTER THREE

Ah, hell no, Monica. Please tell me Courtland didn't do that to you. I know that convertible-Mercedes-Benz-flaunting, Double-Platinum-American-Express-Card-waving, everybody-need-to-know-my-family-name brotha ain't that damn trifling. Girl, you need to stop playing with me, 'cause if you sure 'nuff telling the truth, then you need to refocus and forget about cutting him off. Instead you need come up with a plan to cut *it* off."

Theresa is my girl, and I know that she has my back, but she just can't leave her ghetto past behind her. She is right, though. Courtland has given me a bad case of the crabs. I've been itching and scratching all morning long. When he first talked me into going to dinner with him last night and asked me whether or not I liked crabs, how was I to know that he wasn't just talking about the meal?

"Monica, are you paying me attention? 'Cause you damn sure didn't last night when you were all caught up fantasizing about Courtland being your baby daddy."

With a comment like that, I'm not sure if Theresa is laughing at me or with me, but irregardless, I need someone to talk to, and I know she won't spread my business in the street. As an only child, she's been the closest thing I've had to a sister. We became friends during our freshman year in college. Theresa was street smart and a gifted and talented student, but she had no sense of time and place. I felt like instead of being her roommate, I was her one-on-one guidance counselor, fashion consultant, as well as her own personal upward mobility Jack and Jill self-help guru and motivational speaker. My parents wanted me to change roommates the moment they realized that the girl outside the dorm cursing up a storm and threatening to hit a guy upside the head with an empty 40-ounce malt liquor bottle was none other than my roommate and newly found best friend, Theresa Hall. According to them, they weren't paying all that money for me to go to college to be exposed to the ghetto slum life that they had spent so much time trying to keep me away from.

What my parents didn't know was that during my first semester in college, an upperclassman who was popular on the yard had taken an interest in me and had subsequently drugged me and tried to date rape me at an off-campus party. If it had not been for Theresa becoming worried when I didn't answer her instant messages or phone calls and deciding to come back to the party to look for me, I would have been sexually assaulted. She took the initiative to find out where the guy who drugged me lived off campus, and when Theresa arrived and saw my car parked in front of his building, she relentlessly banged on his apartment door until he finally opened it.

The effects of the date rape drug had made me totally woozy and delirious. I was barely conscious and couldn't maintain my balance. It was difficult to tell the difference between being awake and dreaming. I struggled to make out all the words Theresa was saying to him that night with her head spinning

18

around as if on the Matrix, but I do remember the words, "I'll cut cha," and with that Theresa somehow managed to get me out of his apartment, down the steps, and into her car. When we got back to the dorm, I eventually came back to normal. Several hours later, I recognized that I had more than just a roommate or a college friend, I had someone who had my back like the sister I dreamed of.

"Monica, my husband and I are going to brunch after church. Would you like to join us for a crab sandwich, crab cakes or crab hors d'oeuvres?"

"That's not funny. You see me here in dire straits and all you have are condescending jokes."

"Girl, I have your back. I'm just playing. I know you know how much I care for you. I was just surprised that you would have cared or liked someone like Courtland. I know you can do better. When did my girl, the poster child for Black independent women, all of a sudden become so superficial?"

"You just don't get it. Even an independent woman such as myself needs male companionship every once in a while. I can't help it if I am attracted to good lookin', successful, high profilin', charming men. For one reason or another, I thought Courtland was Mr. Right."

"Yeah, you mean Mr. Right Now."

Shifting my position on the sofa, I said, "Theresa, you are so blessed to be married to a wonderful man who wants to be a man. It is almost impossible nowadays to meet a heterosexual man who has his act together. When a man cheats on you today, you don't know if it's with Christine or Christopher."

"That down-low thing is a mess."

"I don't know who to trust. It seems like men are coming out of the closet on a regular basis."

"Yes, they are. Girl, did you hear what happened at First Central Church?"

Theresa hit a sensitive nerve. While Theresa had recently begun attending First Central Church, it has been my church for several years. I've been active in several ministries. If there is one thing that everybody knows, you better not say anything negative about my church or my pastor. I have ended many acquaintances and quasi-friendships the moment someone said something bad about First Central.

I have been going back and forth throughout the past five years in an emotionally-abusive and sometimes physically-abusive relationship. Despite being a college graduate and a woman who has dreams for the future, my ex-boyfriend, Marcus, had a way of making me feel like I was nothing and was nobody. My self-esteem had reached continually new all-time lows. My sense of self-worth was continuing to go down on a daily basis while my calorie intake was going up. I had put on twenty-two pounds of depression which resulted in him saying that I was becoming fat and ugly and that if I kept it up, not only would he not want me anymore, but nobody else would either.

I felt emotionally trapped and unable to cope with life. It became a chore just to get up in the morning and face life. I had a book of alibis for the physical scars I carried on my face and body. I fell down the steps; I tripped on the sidewalk; I walked into a door. You name the scar and accident, and I had an excuse for how it got there. I felt invisible and that no one understood my tribulations. I was walking in and out of life because I had to in order to survive. How was I going to escape this daily pain that I felt and the man who helped put it there? I needed a plan, and I needed it fast.

My girlfriends tried to encourage me by having a "girls' night in" where we laid around the living room eating and drinking while discussing, gossiping and demoralizing the existence of men. Then, the occasional Girls' Night Out turned into everyday happy hours filled with the same crowd from the night before moving from one restaurant or club to the next. We were becoming the common crowd formerly known as the popular crowd. It was disgusting. Dirty old men begging to be your sugar daddy; young men without a pot to piss in nor a window to throw it out of promising you a lifestyle that they didn't have, and sistas desperately trying not to look too available but secretly begging for an invite to dance and whatever comes thereafter. The only decent part of the evening was the music and the drinks, and that was even skeptical at times. It was the same scenario being played out night after night.

I had gotten it down to a science. There was Margarita Mondays, Champagne Tuesdays, Open Mic Wednesdays, Karaoke Thursdays, and of course, White Linen Fridays. No matter what day of the week I went out with the girls, by the weekend I still felt unfulfilled, weak, and there was still no end to my pain.

When a lady from my job invited me to an upcoming First Central Women's Conference retreat entitled, "Women of Power, Purpose and Prosperity," I initially declined. I didn't see how being with a bunch of church ladies was going to help me in any way, at least that's what I thought. Through persistence and a lot of coaxing, I reluctantly accepted the invitation. It was the most therapeutic, life-altering weekend of empowerment that I had ever experienced. For the first time in a long time, my tears and crying were not an expression of sadness, but rather of the hope that I have for myself in life. I felt renewed and refreshed. Tons of frustration, disappointment and self-doubt that I had been allowing to take root and harvest within me were being replaced with a feeling of self-value and significance. I reclaimed my dignity and decided at that conference that I was going to take control of my life, cut that zero named Marcus and make God and my church first in my life.

So you can understand how hurt I was when I heard that a woman in my Sunday school class named Alexis Benson, whose engagement party I had attended and who was scheduled to get married in St. Thomas, had recently found out that her fiancé, Derrick, had been cheating on her. It was several months later when I found out that during the period they were seeking marriage counseling, her fiancé had been secretly having sex with someone else. What made the situation so hard to overcome was that the affair was with the associate minister providing their marriage counseling. The minister had also slept with many other fiancés while being privately diagnosed as HIV-positive, and he was engaging in sex with both men and women. Allegedly unbeknownst to the senior pastor and church leadership, the minister had been discreetly counseling on a one-on-one basis people who were considering marriage and encouraging them to explore their sexual curiosity and inhibitions before they got married in order to remove the sexual temptations and desires. The associate minister promised to keep everything confidential and would even serve as a personal assistant to their sexual urges because he lied and said he could pray it all away for them. He secretly recorded some male and female parishioners, who were contemplating marriage, having sex with him, while he blackmailed others to have sex with him based upon the information that he learned from their sessions.

According to Alexis, her fiancé Derrick's cell phone seemed to be ringing a lot and having an abnormal amount of incoming calls on it. One night while he was asleep, she checked his cell and saw that all of these text messages and missed calls were from their marriage counselor. Alexis wondered why he wasn't also calling her out of concern. She hadn't heard from the associate minister since their last meeting, and he had needed to reschedule the last two counseling sessions.

Feeling guilty about having pre-marital sex, Alexis had promised herself that the current box of condoms that her fiancé had in his bedroom dresser drawer would be the last box, and then they would abstain until marriage. Whenever Alexis went over to Derrick's condo and he was out of the bedroom, she meticulously recounted the number of condoms in the box. When Alexis had last checked the box of condoms, she found two condoms instead of the four as previously counted. Immediately, Alexis burst into tears. She was certain that the amount should be four. Alexis needed someone to talk to and knew that her fiancé Derrick was supposed to be in marriage counseling that night at the church. Driving frantically and in need of an explanation, she made it to the church.

Everyone meeting at the First Central Church had basically left for the night leaving only Derrick's car, the custodian, the security guard and the associate minister. During the last several weeks,

Alexis felt that too many women had been giving her fiancé too many inappropriate, congratulatory hugs, and she was becoming uncomfortable with it. When she approached Derrick last week concerning the matter, he assured Alexis that it was innocent and that he only loved her and no other woman.

Derrick didn't lie about her being the only woman he desired. But unbeknownst to her, he also desired men.

When Alexis reached the associate minister's office, the door was closed. Yet, she could still hear a voice that sounded like Derrick's saying, "I don't want to leave Alexis. It would hurt her, and I love her, but I am in love with you."

Alexis burst through the door only to find Derrick embraced in the arms of the associate minister. She felt shocked and betrayed and wanted to hurt Derrick for breaking her heart, as well as hurt the associate minister for misusing her trust. She went to throw something at him from off his desk, but instead the realization that her fiancé had been kissing the associate minister made her want to throw up. Alexis said that she became suddenly dizzy and almost passed out.

More important than hurting Derrick or the associate minister, she wanted to run into the sanctuary and fall before the altar and beg God not to give her AIDS. Alexis had broken her promise not to have premarital sex anymore when she met Derrick. Now the reminder of a sermon that she had heard from a visiting pastor, the Reverend Doctor David Josiah Goodwell, was firmly in her mind as she grasped her Bible and fell prostrate on the church carpet. Pastor Goodwell had said, "You can make choices to have protected sex or unprotected sex, but there is no such thing as protected sin."

It turned out that Derrick and the associate minister had been secretly having an affair for several weeks. Derrick wanted to marry Alexis initially to hide his secret sex life but fell in love with her in the process. There were still unresolved issues concerning his attraction to men that he was trying to work through. It turned out that his hidden gay lifestyle stemmed back to early issues in his childhood with having been molested.

What disappointed Alexis and many women such as me in the church is that it is hard to know whether a man is truly heterosexual or not. My decision to have sex with Courtland on the first night was clearly a poor choice that has had a lot of consequences. In a desperate attempt to get a man who wanted a woman and whose socio-economic variables look good on paper, I increased my sexuality and lowered my standards. It would have been bad enough for Courtland to play mind games with me, break my heart and have me wanting to not leave the house, but he took it to another level and gave me crabs to go.

It has been alleged that many women in First Central Church had been propositioned but didn't tell anyone until Alexis went ballistic over what happened to her. Nobody wanted to be the first to make such a negative claim against such a popular minister who was very influential. The associate minister and the minister of music were good friends in and out of church, and that should have been a clue for all of us since the minister of music's alternative lifestyle and feminine characteristics were well-known or alleged. According to Alexis, the minister of music threatened to leave if the associate minister was disciplined based upon uncorroborated accusations. Both the associate minister and Derrick deny that anything happened between them. Personally, I don't know what to believe. I just know that First Central has been good to me, and I won't let anybody bring down my church or my pastor.

"Oh, my God. Theresa, are you watching the news?"

"Why?"

"Turn to Channel 25 quickly. You're not going to believe what just flashed across the screen."

CHAPTER FOUR

A s the minister of music of Mount Caramel Baptist Church, Reverend Reginald Walker had the privilege of introducing to our church family on numerous occasions a host of different renowned Grammy and Stellar Award gospel artists, but never have I ever heard him speak of a majestic soprano voice that he could imagine would cause for the angels in heaven to stop singing, look towards Earth and through the splendor of our church's stained glass windows, shake their heads while uttering the words, 'My, my, my. That child can sing.'

"That is why, as your pastor, it is my privilege to introduce to you for the first time a rich blend of traditional and contemporary gospel sound that many have said is unmatched outside of Heaven. Join me in welcoming a very special guest, the incomparable De'Borah Harriston."

I watched De'Borah gracefully make her way from the roped off second row, center pew to the front of the two-hundred-forty-member choir loft as parishioners on both the balcony and main level of the sanctuary gave a warm greeting of applause. When she arrived at the stage, she paused before the microphone and waited until she could feel every single eye throughout the congregation focused solely on her. De'Borah then glanced towards me in the pulpit and then to the organist before preparing to showcase her six-octave range with a classic soulful acappella rendition of "Great is Thy Faithfulness." De'Borah had barely sung one note and already the entire Mount Caramel Baptist Church was standing on its feet admiring the elegance, richness and beauty of her voice as she hit one high note after another.

Prior to my dad, the Honorable Reverend Cecil Douglass Goodwell, passing away, I thought the greatest challenge I would ever face in life would be living up to his expectations as his eldest son. When you have a father whose legacy as a minister and politician made him loved and adored by the church congregation and the community at-large, the family legacy weighs on your heart heavy. After finally accepting Jesus Christ as Lord and Savior, acknowledging my own calling to preach and completing my seminary degree, I found myself within a span of months reluctantly joining the staff of my dad's church, only to have him die shortly after and the trustee board appoint me to lead one of the most prominent congregations in the city.

Every day I deal with the reality that many pastors, not only in my city but throughout the nation, not only want to be where I am, but are envious of where I am at. Mount Caramel Baptist has thousands of members who unquestionably love the church and would do anything for Mount Caramel. I have come to understand that there is a place for that type of love in some measured regards, but I'm deeply concerned that many of the parishioners of Mount Caramel Baptist have *churchianity* versus Christianity. They have an extensive, meaningful and deep relationship with church, but not necessarily a relationship with Christ. There are a lot of people who are members or attendees of my church but knowingly and unknowingly have never become disciples of

Christ. They appear not to know or are indifferent to the fact that the church can't forgive their sins nor save their souls; only Jesus can.

In the years since I left home after college, it appears that my father, in an attempt to keep up with the Joneses in the pulpit and remain relevant in a materialistic, self-indulgent, decadent society, decided he would build his own multi-million dollar lifestyle and new church edifice, which is as mammoth as a coliseum, through compromising and watering down the gospel with sermons that promised materialistic prosperity and preyed on the fragile broken hearts of countless women who wanted and needed for someone to believe in them. So they believed in Reverend Cecil Goodwell more than they believed in God.

I have come to understand that while it is definitely true that God never gives you more than you can bear and that God does not give a person a responsibility, mission, ministry or vision unless God has a plan of provision so that the objectives that God would want to see come true are brought to life, I agonize over the daunting task of having to tear down and destroy the bulk of everything my father built, including my family name, as I attempt to preach and teach the truth about Jesus to a congregation that ultimately may prefer the sugar water, non-substantive, carefree, no accountability to God gospel that causes for church membership to grow, but not the people in it.

A soul-stirring rendition of one of my favorite gospel songs by a church elder who followed after Ms. De'Borah Harriston's sparkling performance has everyone shouting and praising the name of God. Yokes are being broken. Shackles of depression and guilt are falling off faster than tears streaming down the faces of both men and women. The presence of the Lord clearly has entered the room in the way that causes several choir members to jump up and down in the air praising Jesus Christ as Lord and Savior and others just to fall on the ground and worship the Lord with truth, power and conviction. In the midst of all the screams of "Hallelujah. Glory be to God," I receive a note from Maurice, Chairman of the Deacon Board, concerning an urgent message left by Crystal Calloway saying:

"DJ, it is an emergency. I am at the North Side police precinct and have to raise a million dollar bond. I desperately need your help. I wouldn't come to you unless I had to. Don't let me down. It's connected to the death of your parishioner, Evelyn James. Please hurry."

CHAPTER FIVE

S everal hours ago, Evelyn and I were both pregnant. She was pregnant with my grandchild, me with anger. Evelyn and the baby are unfortunately dead, and I'm still pregnant. No longer with anger, but instead with fear, trying my best not to give birth to despair.

I can still hear the sounds of multiple police car sirens blaring in my quiet, upscale cul-de-sac. The strobe lights penetrating the Venetian blinds zigzagged throughout the foyer into the expansive remodeled sunken living room creating a bizarre laser light show that caught my attention, but not as much as the police officers swarming my early nineteenth century historic colonial-style home. From every direction you could imagine, police officers screamed orders to "come out with your hands up in the air." The brutal murder of runway model Evelyn James had made the lead story and special report on every radio and television station in the city.

I had meticulously removed any level of evidence that could remotely connect me to the scene of Ms. James's killing. The police bursting through my custom-made French doors was a complete shock only to be out done by the arrest and charging of my son, Shelton, with the murder of Evelyn James.

Shelton's deep baritone voice screaming, "Mommy, I didn't do it…What are they talking about?…I didn't kill anybody.…What's going on?" was lot for me to handle. I was in total, complete shock and still processing the fact that the police, outfitted in full storm trooper riot gear, had invaded my home with enough fire power to carry out a third world nation coup.

The sight of the police placing handcuffs around my son's wrists was enough to make me almost want to confess on the spot. I had to suppress the motherly urge to say, "I'm the one you're looking for, not my son," and instead see the wonderful opportunity that his arrest was for both of us.

Shelton had lived a privileged life to the point where he didn't have a great enough appreciation for how hard fought were the gains my husband Steven and I had made against enormous obstacles. Shelton was born with movie star looks, a photogenic smile and charm to match. His notoriety prior to tonight's arrest resulted from his six-foot-eight body frame, long arm wingspan, soft touch jump shot, penetrating quick step off the dribble and an over 40-inch vertical that propelled him into a dominating 31.2 points, 14 rebounds, 11.5 assists per game high school prodigy and soon to be NBA phenomenon.

A formidable frontcourt and backcourt player, Shelton had led his high school team to back-to-back State championships during his sophomore and junior years. However, to the dismay of school administrators and certain political officials, I took Shelton out of school during the beginning of his senior year and decided to home school him. In light of the network of college graduates and professionals in the variety of fields that was a part of our family circle, I didn't feel that the quality of the education that he was receiving at his school was commiserate to the expectations that

Steven and I had for him. Shelton was a very bright student with solid good grades. In light of the enormous amount of traveling that Shelton was doing with basketball tournaments and the long hours he was spending in practice and watching game film, I noticed a dramatic reduction in his academic studying time, and there seemed very little honor in his making the honor roll. As a concerned parent who valued education, it was my responsibility to make sure that the high quality expectations that my husband and I had set were reflected in the quality of instruction and type of learning environment that he was in.

When my husband and I announced that Shelton would not be playing basketball this season, there was an enormous amount of outrage by the local community and school administrators who had leased a 15,000-seat college basketball coliseum to host the school's home games. Licensing and sales of school paraphernalia had reached astronomical proportions, and there was a lucrative, undisclosed, high figure deal that had been struck by the school and a leading cable network to televise Shelton's home and away games.

People were making truck loads of money in the millions off my son, and due to various archaic rules, we were not eligible to receive any of it. When I had first inquired prior to the start of the basketball season about what provisions were being made for small and minority-owned businesses to compete for various contracts as primary agents or subcontractors, I was informed by school officials and other business entities that the information I was requesting was a confidential matter and was out of my purview as a parent.

A well-orchestrated campaign to discredit me and my husband

was launched when it was determined that we would not rescind from our position concerning Shelton playing basketball during this season. This past year, our home life has been riveted by constant, daily battles between my husband and I and our teenage son over what was best for him as well as our attempts to reign in his growing level of blatantly disrespectful, rude and inappropriate behavior towards us. People, including several coaches, have masqueraded as his so-called friends and have done a thorough job of convincing him that we have been conspiring to ruin his life and were jealous of his future earning potential and stardom.

A boycott of my husband Steven's latest independent film had been launched online as well as pressure was put on several of his business partners to relinquish their investments in Steven's film and video projects—all due to our removing Shelton from playing basketball—and if they didn't disavow their association with Calloway Enterprises, they could expect to lose future substantial state contracts. Out of the blue, my name began to appear in the city's main newspaper connecting me to an investigation concerning a ruthless drug dealer and aspiring hip-hop artist named "Prince Murda."

My husband and I had taken a lot of negative press and had to bear the brunt for protecting Shelton against negative outside influences. This temporary situation of his being charged with murder will be a great learning lesson for him in regards to who really cares about him, especially since the endorsements were undoubtedly going to be drying up and people who have had only their selfish reasons for knowing my son will be trying to disassociate themselves from him. Through the false murder charges against my son, I can prove to Shelton that all the people he thinks care for him don't, while using this unfortunate situation to reclaim the closeness of our loving family during the possible upcoming trial as well as make it so that neither one of us ever has to spend a day in jail.

I'm not going to let my child be convicted of a crime that he didn't commit, but if I have a way to possibly avoid both of us going to prison and keeping my family intact, then I'm going to pursue it. If raising the bail money causes for me to have to contact my brother-in-law, the man Steven can't stand, in order to help get our son out of jail, then that's something Steven and I are going to have to deal with.

The Reverend Doctor David Josiah Goodwell was family. In light of the allegations by certain Mount Caramel Baptist Church members that DJ was having or had had a possible affair with his parishioner Evelyn James, the same woman who I thought Steven had had an affair with, I concluded that the voluptuous vixen was trying to bamboozle all of the most influential men in the city. With DJ's favorite nephew being charged with her murder, I was certain that he would respond to the urgent message I sent through his church secretary. I know that with all his preaching about God and the importance of family, he is not going to leave us to fend for ourselves when he could help out. Technically, I would have thought he would be here by now, but look, ah here, speak of the devil—or should I say in the case of Reverend Goodwell, speak of the angel—look who just walked through a parade of reporters into the police precinct.

Reverend Goodwell greeted me with a concerned look and close yet awkward hug, "Crystal, I thought you were locked up. What's going on? I've been listening to different news reports on my way coming down. How can I help?"

"DJ, thank you for responding to my note. I recognize that I sent it to you during the middle of your pastoral anniversary church service, so I appreciate you coming down here as fast as you did."

"Crystal, I just want to be helpful. You know how much I love Shelton."

"If it wasn't for you being so loving by introducing Shelton to Evelyn at the fundraiser last year, my baby wouldn't even be in this situation. You got nerve turning your leftover hoochies over to your nephew."

"You are way out of line, Crystal."

"No, you were out of line, DJ, by having an affair and then turning your mistress on to Shelton."

"I didn't come down here for this. I never had an affair with Ms. James and am insulted by your accusations. All I want to know is, how much money do you need from me to help get Shelton out of jail? Where is Steven, or is he even here?"

"Steven is not here. He is away on a video shoot in Jamaica and won't be able to catch a flight in until tomorrow morning. I don't want my Shelton to have to spend one more minute in jail than he has to. There are a lot of crazy, vindictive people out here who would love to hurt my baby."

"You still haven't told me how much money you need?"

"I need $400,000."

"That's a lot of money, Crystal. I am a pastor, not a pimp. I'll have to speak to Vanessa before I can commit to something like that."

"Since when did DJ need someone else's approval before making decisions?"

"I don't need anyone else's approval. I'm talking about consulting my wife. Never mind that. What have you been able to find out concerning why the police suspect Shelton of murdering Evelyn?"

"So she's Evelyn now."

"Evelyn, Ms. James, whatever. Crystal, just tell me what you have been able to find out."

"So far the case against Shelton is primarily circumstantial. If the District Attorney pursues this case, and in light of the high level of publicity, I am certain that she will, I believe that it's beatable."

"Are you saying Shelton killed her?"

"No. What I am saying is that there was enough evidence to warrant questioning him and perhaps arresting him, but they didn't have to do it the way that they did. I don't believe for one moment that Shelton killed her. I totally believe him when he says that he is innocent."

I then took a deep breath, looked around the police precinct corridor to make sure that nobody could overhear me and slowly let it out. "It appears that that hoochie Evelyn James was having sex with Shelton in the hopes of cashing in on him when he joins the NBA."

"I can't believe it," responded Reverend Goodwell.

"What? You can't believe that she was a ho or that Shelton was sleeping with her? Because if anyone should know about the whorish part, you should."

Tired of the false accusations but still prayerfully desiring to help and do the work of God, Reverend Goodwell said, "Crystal,

I told you before. I don't wanna hear any more lies about me and Evelyn. Just tell me whatever else you have been able to uncover."

"Well, I was able to pull a couple of favors from friends of mine on the force and learned that they brought her husband, Rodney, in for questioning and that he had an alibi that pretty much excludes him from the scene of the murder. It doesn't mean that he might not have played a part in it, it just means that based upon what they've learned so far that it is unlikely that he could have pulled the trigger. But I still wouldn't put anything past him."

"Crystal, you still haven't explained to me why they charged Shelton."

"Well, for one, he lied to the police when they asked him about his relationship with Ms. James. And I just don't get that. For the life of me, I can't figure out why the boy would answer any questions from the police at all," I said, tossing my hands up in frustration. "He definitely knows better than that, and I've definitely taught him better than that. But he just went on and did things his way anyhow. Now look what happened. He done told the police that he only knew Evelyn as a friend while the police already had evidence that confirmed otherwise and were just waiting for him to lie about anything."

Reverend Goodwell expressed his sorrow by shaking his head and looking towards Heaven.

"But what really has Shelton jammed up, DJ, are the phone calls he made. According to my contact, Shelton called Evelyn at least twenty-two times in just one hour during today. His messages fluctuated from 'I love you' to 'I can't stand you' to 'I can't live without you' to 'Is the kid really mine?' to 'I don't want this to end.' "

"Evelyn was pregnant?" It was more than just a question from Reverend Goodwell, but a statement of shock.

"As sad as that sounds, it's true. I spoke to Steven just before you got here, and he confirmed that he met with Evelyn in-person before he flew out to Jamaica. It turns out that Steven and Shelton had decided on their own that it was better that I didn't know about the pregnancy until they figured out if the child was Shelton's or not."

"Wow."

"All you have to say is, 'Wow'?"

"This is just a lot to absorb, Crystal. Just give me a moment." After a few seconds, Reverend Goodwell asked, "Are the police considering Steven as a possible suspect?"

"They are and have, but according to what I've been hearing here in the precinct, it doesn't seem possible that Steven could have changed clothes so fast before boarding the plane for Jamaica. I know this much, it doesn't help his situation that she was murdered and he left the country soon after."

"Do you think the police are planning to arrest him?"

"Not from what I can gather. Steven volunteered on his own to return back to the States immediately. He told me that he answered all of their questions and didn't feel that he was in jeopardy, but who knows nowadays. All I know is that they got my baby Shelton locked up for murder, and I believe with all of my heart that he is innocent."

"I believe Shelton, too. There has to be more to this than what you've been able to find out if the police are holding Shelton for murder."

"There is, DJ. I just don't like repeating it."

"And what might that be?"

I paused and looked Reverend Goodwell square in the eyes before taking a slow deep breath. My eyelids closed softly. Within a matter of seconds tears started flowing down my cheeks. Gingerly, I placed both of my hands in front of my face as though they were a mask or some type of shield to fend away or hide my growing vulnerability. After a few uneven sighs, Dr. Goodwell placed his hand on my shoulder and told me, "It's going to be all right."

I replied in the softest, most fragile voice I could muster, "I don't know, DJ. They have a telephone recording of Shelton saying, 'I will kill you if you don't pick up the damn phone.' "

I burst out in tears. The broad arms of Pastor Goodwell's warm Christian embrace became my sanctuary while I continued concocting a plan that could send me straight to hell.

CHAPTER SIX

The streets have spoken. It's official. The hottest radio station in the city hosted by yours truly, DJ Exclusive, is now home to the new #1 most listened to radio program in the country. To all my listeners out there, you made this possible. When they said it couldn't be done, you made it happen. In less than one year, we took this radio station from #15 in the city to now #1 in the country. So I tell you what I'm going to do. The fifteenth caller to the station right now is going to receive backstage passes and front row tickets to the biggest, baddest, sold-out concert of the year. But I won't stop there. I'm sending you to the hottest concert of the year in true baller status. You and your guest will be picked up in a customized Mercedes Benz chauffeured limousine, taken on a $5,000 shopping spree earlier in the evening, and later on that night after the concert, you will join me and my posse of celebrity stars for platinum VIP-status treatment at an undisclosed concert after-party that is so exclusive, we can't even announce where it's going to happen. All you need to know is that you as the fifteenth caller to the #1 rated radio station in the country will be in the house. But it doesn't stop there. I'm going to give you $10,000 in crisp $100 bills so you can get your groove on. That's right. Ten thousand dollars. Call me right now at 555-H-O-T-T. That's right. 555-HOTT.

"Wait. Wait. Wait. Wait a minute. Before we begin the call-in, I got a special guest on the line. This is the reason why other radio stations hate us and you, the greatest listeners in the world, love us. Live on the radio, right now on the DJ Exclusive Show is the youngin' with the fastest certified gold hip-hop album ever, the one and only Prince Murda. What is going on Prince Murda?"

"Yeah. Yeah. Yeah. What's up, fam?"

"I'm holding it down. Thanks for coming on my show. Before I begin asking you any questions, Prince, I want to congratulate you on your instant hip-hop classics, *Your Girl, My Ho* and *Grindin' 'Til We Die*. The songs are blazing. Did you know that the streets would be feeling you like that?"

"Naw, I can't say that I knew for a fact, but I did feel when I was in the studios that I had something special. I just didn't know if I would get enough spins on the stations for people to hear it, you know what I'm saying."

"I can respect that."

"You've been in this business for awhile, DJ Exclusive, so you know where I'm coming from when I say the politics in this music industry is cold vicious. Straight ruthless. That is why I definitely appreciate your showing love and having me on your show. It means a lot. To everyone out there who be blasting my music from the streets to the suites, I want to say thank you and one luv for all your support. Thanks for holding a brotha down. And without a doubt, I wanna give special thanks and special props to the man above. None of this would be possible without God."

"Check this out. Prince Murda, my listeners would go craaazzzy if I had you on the air and didn't ask you what is up with the television footage being shown on Channel 25, and probably by now on every other television station, showing you running out of a club with a gun in your hand. What the hell happened? There are so many rumors going on. All that anyone knows is five people got shot: three which are dead, two in critical condition, and you have a warrant out for your arrest."

"I really can't speak on that right now. I will tell you, don't believe everything you hear."

"Can my listeners and I believe everything we see?"

"Naw. Just hold off on that for a minute. I will get back with you on that."

"Well how about this. Is it true, Prince Murda, that your hit single Your Girl, My Ho was directed at NBA-bound high school player Shelton Calloway and his relationship with video model Evelyn James? There are large numbers of people who are saying that Shelton killed Evelyn James over the fact that she had been secretly sleeping around with you, and you decided to out her and their relationship in your song."

"I'm not claiming that. The song never mentioned him by name, but if he took it that way, then that's on him."

"Listeners are instant messaging the studio asking me, Prince Murda, are you denying reports that an altercation between yourself and Shelton Calloway, aka Killa C, didn't occur after Evelyn was caught coming out of your trailer half-dressed during a video shoot for the lead single on your album *Body Count—Taking No Prisoners*?"

"No, I'm not denying that some words were said, but all the gossip about guns being drawn, tables being overturned and people threatening to kill somebody is totally untrue. None of it happened. Do you hear me? None of it happened."

"So, Prince Murda, are you confirming for us that you were sexing her and you kicked her out of your trailer half-naked when she told you that she may be pregnant with your kid?"

"I really can't speak on this, but I will say this. She wasn't in the trailer to see me. Period. She's dead. I didn't kill her. People are trying to make this about hip-hop, but it's not. It's way bigger than that. Evelyn's death is political, and that's all I got to say on that. Don't ask me no more questions about her. Move to another subject."

CHAPTER SEVEN

Jordan, what the hell is this?" screamed Theresa dangling a Victoria Secret thong in the air recently removed from my worn-torn travel suitcase. Not knowing how to respond to my wife, I just stared at the red satin-laced panty with a bewildered look on my face that said, "I don't know what you're talking about."

"Jordan, do you hear me? What the hell is this?"

"A thong," I responded matter of factly.

"Who the hells is it, and what is it doing in your suitcase?" was not only a question/statement by Theresa Hall but it was accompanied by some of the best neck and eye rolling motions ever choreographed by a Black woman of any age. All of her body gyrations and facial expressions were comical and hilarious to me in what undoubtedly was a very serious moment for both of us, because whether I recognized it or not, her comments, tone of voice and posturing were all the signs of an angry woman who was preparing to go to war.

"Theresa, listen to me clearly. As strange as this may sound, I don't know whose thong it is or where it came from, and if I didn't see you unzip the suitcase myself and pull it out, I would have thought that you were lying about it or making it up."

"You have got to be kiddin'. Are you saying you don't have no answers or there is no need for an explanation?"

"No, Theresa. I don't."

"The hell you don't. You need to come up with an answer or something," continued a shouting Theresa as she stared coldly at me with a volatile mixture of contempt, disbelief and hurt.

"Theresa, I really don't know what to tell you. All I can say is that I am not cheating on you and I haven't done anything wrong."

"Jordan, that is totally unacceptable," barked an irate Theresa while pacing back and forth around the room.

"No, what is unacceptable, Theresa, is your bombarding me with all these damn questions that I don't know the answers for. If I did have any answers, I would have told you a long time ago. There is no reason for me to lie to you."

"Jordan, I'm gonna help you out since you claim that you are clueless," Theresa began as she slammed the bedroom door and positioned herself between me and the 56-inch plasma TV while yelling at a feverish high pitch. "What is the name of the heifer that you were with last night that caused for you not to return the ten messages I left for you?"

"Woman, you are getting on my damn nerves. Leave me the hell alone with this nonsense. If I said I didn't do anything, then I didn't do anyth. If said I don't know where the thong came from, then that is exactly what I meant. I don't know."

"Jordan, don't get it twisted. Whether I found panties or not, don't think for a moment that we weren't going to have a discussion about why you didn't answer your phone. I was just waiting for the appropriate time to bring it up without an argument, but your dumb behind is so trifling or don't give a damn that you packed the trick's underwear you were with in your luggage."

46

Theresa tightly balled the red thong up in her fist and threw it straight at my head with a bold vengeance that clearly said, "I can't stand you, and I wish we had never met." She then followed up her actions with, "By the way, Jordan, I called your hotel front desk at 3 a.m. in the morning when I couldn't get you on the hotel phone and was informed by the clerk that you were not in your room but on your way back upstairs via the elevators. But here is the catch. I lied and asked if my sister was with you because I was trying to get in contact with her. The clerk told me that yes, both of you were heading to your hotel room, but here is the hook. I don't have no sister. So who the hell were you with?"

I was unaware until then that she had called that many times. Since the conversation began, my focus was on totally refuting and rebutting all the unfounded allegations that Theresa had been lodging at me. I wasn't the least bit concerned about exonerating myself for something I hadn't done, nor had I focused any energy on evaluating how the thong got into my suitcase. I knew I had spent the last several days in frantic business meetings with corporate CEOs raising campaign funds for the upcoming presidential elections.

But when Theresa said something about a woman being in my hotel suite, it suddenly hit me what had happened.

During the previous evening, I had determined that instead of going to some of the numerous raucous Hollywood after-parties being held in different suites throughout the five-star hotel, I would spend a little bit of time networking in the hotel lounge bar before retiring to my room for some well-deserved R&R. Sensitive to the thin line between being courteous, friendly and flirtatious, I mingled with a host of established lobbyists, political

47

operatives and gurus as well as renowned media consultants from different political candidates throughout the country attending the conference.

When a college buddy I had not seen in years showed up and introduced me to his new attractive bride and their friends, we immediately began to reminisce about the good old days when we used to believe that politics was about ideas and service versus money and favors.

I eventually confided with him during a private conversation on the way to the bar to get more drinks that I was still struggling with my decision to politically join forces with the frontrunner, an opportunistic white woman presidential candidate with a hidden political and social agenda, rather than siding with the intelligent, charismatic Black male presidential candidate who appeared to be a chameleon with blind ambition.

After sharing countless college horror stories of campaigning door-to-door for local and national candidates as well as the endless hours we spent working phone banks, we decided that some of us wanted to skip the loud, alcohol-crazed environment we were in so we could watch the highly-touted rematch between the most-feared boxers in the middle weight division and re-live our old spades rivalry.

Once up in the hotel room, I sensed a certain level of unhealthy eye contact between myself and the newlywed, but I tried to discount it to the alcohol I had been drinking as well as to some misinterpretation of the signals she was possibly inadvertently sending me.

In the midst of boxing match touted by some newscasters as the fight of the decade, my college buddy asked to use my laptop computer to confirm his airline flight time as well as to print out his boarding pass. The wireless connection wasn't working properly on the laptop, so we hooked up the computer the prehistoric way with the phone land line. A sudden shriek from one of the spades players refocused everyone's attention to the television screen for a mutual chorus of boos and accusations that the championship fight was fixed.

After hours of competitive spades, telling witty and hilarious jokes about each other that would make even the most conservative, stoic person fall to the ground with belly-aching laughter, the number of people in my hotel suite had dwindled from eight to four—my college buddy, his flirtatious new wife, her friend and me.

With so few people surrounding us to deflect the attention, I was really starting to feel uncomfortable with the idea of being accused of flirting with a recently married woman, but it was becoming harder and harder to resist the combination of her beauty, sultry voice, adulterous playful comments and glances. I decided to focus my attention on the associate of hers she had invited to join us to play spades. My goal was to covertly flirt with her spades partner in a way that implied that I had an interest in getting to know her sexually. My hope was that when the married woman observed my actions, she would feel insulted by my new-found interest in her colleague and that it would deter her from flirting with me since my college buddy might detect that as a married man I was engaged in a form of foreplay with his wife and his wife's friend. My plan worked too well.

Within minutes, the woman's toes were slowing making there way up of the inner part of my leg, stroking both my calf muscle and my ego simultaneously before resting on the soft part of my thigh. Torn by the sensuality of her touch and the desires it was creating in me, I excused myself away from the table to get something to drink. In the interim, the bride expressed her desire to leave my hotel room and get some much needed rest before the new day.

As her husband escorted her to the door, I took it upon myself to walk the three of them out of my suite. It was at that time that I learned that the other woman was not staying in the hotel but at a nearby trendy bed and breakfast. Whether it was chivalry or a desire to be in her presence for a little longer, I decided to accompany her to the lobby in order to make sure that she was able to acquire a cab.

A stumbling drunkard bent on conversing met us within moments of entering the main rotunda of the lobby. Being inebriated had no bearing on his ability to identify how beautiful the woman walking with me was, so it wasn't a surprise that he felt compelled to share his observations concerning her attractiveness and the elegance with which she strolled.

After inquiring with the desk clerk about the unavailability of taxis at the hotel, we were told that late night clubs were in the process of letting out and therefore cabs throughout the city were all lined up in front of them. Since a taxi would not be available for a long time to come, I decided I would change clothes into something more casual and walk her back to her hotel.

The persistence of the drunkard's awkward advances in wanting to get to know her better had reached the threshold of harassment and border-lined on outright disrespect. The quickest way I knew to bring the annoying behavior to a close was to assert that the woman and I were a couple and his behavior was inappropriate and could lead to a possible but not imminent physical altercation. I felt awkward in leaving her in the lobby with an annoying drunk man so I reluctantly had her accompany me back to my hotel room.

During the elevator ride back up to my room, the lure of the woman remained the same, but my resistance level to her subliminal advances had kicked in. I felt uneasy saying that a woman other than my wife was intimately connected to me. Prior to getting to the room, despite whatever she may have concocted in her mind, I was determined to change into my workout clothes and quickly depart once again from the room. Once we arrived in the hotel suite, I opened up my carryon suitcase that was strategically posted at the door, grabbed my athletic warm-up, went in the bathroom, changed clothes and quickly returned to the living room to inform her that I was ready to go.

By the time I returned, she had already made herself comfortable on the suite's big pillow cushioned sofa, dimmed the lights very low, sprayed some flowery perfume in the air and perhaps on herself, as well as lowered the sound on the television to a whisper before asking me in the most adulterous way whether or not I was sure that I wanted to leave out right now. Without hesitation but remaining courteous, I said, "Definitely," and we left.

It never dawned on me then or in the beginning of the confrontation with my wife that the woman who had last been in my hotel suite had taken off her underwear and placed it in my luggage while I was in the bathroom.

When we arrived back in the lobby, a taxi pulled up to the front door to drop off a cab packed to the max with five people. I immediately made eye contact with the cab driver and told him I had a special tip in store for him if he would be kind enough to drop off my lady companion to her hotel. As soon as it was clear that I would not be escorting her, I could detect a level of disappointment in her mood. While entering the cab, she asked me if I remembered her name. As soon as I said that I didn't remember, she turned red and said, "How could forget so quickly?" I looked at her and said, "I'm sorry. I don't remember, but no need for you to get angry or turn red. I just forgot," to which she replied with a promiscuous smile, "It is not only my skin that is red, and for the record, my name is De'Borah. De'Borah Harriston."

CHAPTER EIGHT

I'm *not going to lie to you. I know what it is like to have sex with someone, wake up in the morning, look over at them and be like, "Damn you're UGLY." But prior to meeting you, I had never, and I do mean never, had that happen after just taking a nap.*

Recognizing the inappropriateness of my comments if actually said out loud to my husband Steven, I instead chose to say to my spouse, "Steven, I love you and have missed you so much. I'm so glad that you made it home safely. Shelton's arrest has been an emotionally taxing experience on me, and it hurts my heart oh so deeply to have the Calloway men in my life whom I love so much being falsely accused of a murder that they didn't commit."

Misty-eyed and fighting back tears, Steven Calloway stood in the middle of our family foyer with a rumpled suit, scruffy beard and unkempt look trying his best not to emotionally break down from the kindness of my words. "Crystal, I don't know what to say about you sometimes. You leave me completely speechless. You're such a wonderful wife and mother, and I just want you to know that I love you more and more each day. I promise you, baby, we as a family are definitely going to come out of this okay."

That was exactly the cue I was looking for to give Steven the biggest syrupy, mushy, romantic hug that anyone could ever muster, while watching him helplessly melt away within my reassuring arms. I then concocted a stream of false tears worthy of any Academy Award-winning actress's best performance before I shared the only truthful words he heard from me all day. "Steven, you and I built this Calloway name and enterprise from scratch, and I will not allow anyone to destroy our family, our family name or any project, endeavor or entity that carries the Calloway name." With that I told him, "Pull it together. Stay strong, and let's work together to clear our son's name."

"Sweetheart, you're oh so right, and I receive that. Matter fact, Crystal, I was thinking about it on the flight home. We can get the money to post bond for Shelton's bail if we get a second mortgage on the house, place our summer home on the market and...."

Deep down I wanted to let Steven go on longer in explaining all the strategies he had been devising to get our baby out of jail, but midway through his proposition, I knew I had already heard enough of his half-baked, ill-conceived capital acquisition bail plans. The irrationality of his suggestions would have exposed the Calloway family name to additional untold ridicule and scorn. All of our so-called friends, acquaintances, business associates and foes would have known that the Calloway's finances weren't nearly as lucrative and substantial as depicted on television and by our glamorous lifestyle. The Calloway image would be unmasked and tarnished before tens of millions of people around the globe. More importantly, we would be vulnerable to our enemies and all who dreamed of our destruction.

So with very little tact, I blurted out, "Steven, I've taken care of it." Based upon the expression on his face, the magnitude of what I said evidently had caught my husband off guard, because for a moment the unthinkable started happening. Steven began pulling away from me. "What do you mean you took care of it?" Unmoved by Steven's inquiry, I replied unemotionally, "Exactly what I said. I took care it."

Steven paused briefly for what seemed like an eternity, uncertain of what to make of my response or what his appropriate follow up should be. He then preceded in a slightly sarcastic tone and body mannerism, "Sweetie, where did you get a million dollars from?"

My response to his questioning was purposefully defensive. I needed to quickly convey to Steven that as my husband, I was majorly disappointed in him as a father. So I dramatically folded both of my arms across my breasts and placed one of those "no he didn't" looks across my face when I said to him, "Steven, I don't get you sometimes. Instead of giving me some strange look of where did I get the money, you should be so overwhelmed with joy that our son is out of jail that all you want to do is jump up and down, run around the room praising God, but instead, you're standing here in my face giving me the fifth degree about where did I raise the bail money from. What the hell is up with that?"

"That's not what I mean, Crystal. I just was surprised you were able to get a hold of that amount of money by yourself."

"Ah, hell no. I know in the midst of all the hell I've been going through, worrying about how to get my baby out of jail, that you are not going to fly in here from some damn video ho shoot in the Caribbean and think you gonna be asking me questions about what steps I've taken to protect our child."

"Crystal, relax. It just caught me off guard, that's all."

"To hell with that. Don't play it down. Ask what you really want to know," I said, agitated. I was on a roll. "If you wanna know whether or not I slept with DJ for the money or if we are having an affair or are seeing each other again, then say so damn it."

"I'm not saying that."

"Are you saying that I've been embezzling money from our company or stealing or hiding money on the side that you didn't know about, then come out and ask me straight. Don't beat around the bush."

"I'm not saying that either."

"Then what the hell are you saying? 'Cause I know what you haven't said, and that is, 'Thank you, baby, for getting our child out of jail. Thank you for worrying about me. Thank you for working hard to clear my name and Shelton's name from a murder. Thank you for all the wonderful public relations you have been working to orchestrate behind the scenes with media contacts, and most importantly, thank you for holding this family down in a time of crisis when I was nowhere to be found."

"You don't have to go there, Crystal. You know exactly where I was."

"That didn't do Shelton or me a damn bit of good."

"Where is Shelton, anyhow?" Steven looked up the spiraling, opulent hallway staircase.

"It's about time you asked about your son."

"Enough already, Crystal. Where is Shelton?" repeated an agitated Steven while walking halfway up the staircase.

"He's at DJ's."

"What?" shouted Steven in mid-stride.

"You ain't deaf. I know you heard me. I said Shelton is at DJ's house. Do you have a problem with that?"

"You know damn well I have a problem with that. Why the hell is he there versus here?"

" 'Cause that is where he wanted to go, Steven." I then walked over to one of the multiple living room bay windows that had thick curtains the length of the window drawn tightly closed to prevent anyone from being able to catch a glimpse of a shadow in our house. With the posture and demeanor of a showgirl preparing to unveil a highly anticipated art figurine, I stood to the side of the bulky curtains and gracefully pulled back a portion of fabric. As expected, countless barrages of camera flashes and photographer strobe lights illuminated the entire living room into a Fourth of July spectacle. With a gentle touch, I released the portion of the curtain I had been holding and then said to Steven, "Do you really wonder why Shelton's not here, or was that a rhetorical question? And before you ask, that is where I got half of the money from for Shelton's bail."

"I can't believe he gave you $500,000."

"Steven, if you are calling me a liar, then we are about to have it out like never before."

"Crystal, it's not that I don't believe that DJ gave it to you. I just wish we didn't need it, 'cause I'm sick and tired of the fact that just because DJ's wife can't have kids he feels like it's okay for him to treat Shelton as though that was his son. Shelton is my son not his, no matter how much they bond together. And frankly, I don't give a damn how much basketball or anything else they have in common. I'm not letting him steal my kid from me."

"Steven, I don't think DJ is trying to steal your kid. The reason

I asked DJ is because we are family now. All of us, Calloways and Goodwells."

"You're not hearing me, woman. So I will say it more clearly. DJ is the last person I want this family to ask one damn thing from."

I was ready to tear into him for raising his voice at me, but his cell phone rang, and he said it was an important business call that he had to take. In reality, the timing was beneficial for both of us. I was tempted to shock the hell out of Steven and share with him information concerning Shelton, as well as the money laundering, prostitution and drug cartel charges facing me in a secret grand jury subpoena that could place us on the front page of every supermarket tabloid and exposé television news show in the world.

A small circle of people in the loop knew that Steven, after graduating from high school, went to California to make a career as an actor, singer, screenwriter and film producer. Nobody, or should I say a very small minority of people in the film industry, was interested in the complex characters and story lines that Steven was trying to get the green light on to be made into films. After a couple of years of receiving tons of rejections, barely making ends meet, and surviving through a variety of minimal jobs, Steven decided to shun the socially-conscious songs and movie scripts and instead devoted his time to capitalizing on the growing urban thug market portrayals that had captured the likes of suburban youth, urban youth, corporate America and global companies from all parts of the world.

Steven knew that with highly-developed artistic skills there were very few things that could stop his independent, low-budget films and videos from being an underground hit and eventually a commercial success. But in order for that to happen, he needed to distance himself from the one thing that reminded him that he would be a failure and disappointment as a person if he was successful in promoting urban thug culture, no matter how much money he made. That one thing was the Goodwell family name, responsibility and reputation. That is why my husband, formerly known and born as Steven Isaiah Goodwell, the brother of David Josiah aka "DJ" Goodwell and the son of the deceased Reverend Doctor Cecil Douglass Goodwell of Mount Caramel Baptist Church, changed his identity and recreated himself in sunny California as the entertainment entrepreneur mogul Steven "Make Money" Calloway.

CHAPTER NINE

Pastor Goodwell, you are tearing this church apart and destroying so much of what took your father so many years to build, and it just breaks my heart deeply on a daily basis. For the life of me, I can't understand why you are ripping our beloved church into pieces," sobbed Deaconess Margaret shaking profusely side-to-side as she reached into her designer leather handbag to acquire a customized embroidered silk handkerchief to wipe away her tears. "I've known you, Pastor, since you were a baby. I knew your mother and your father, God bless their souls. Your father was a great pastor, a wonderful man who was respected and loved by everybody. There's not a day that goes by that everyone in the church doesn't mourn the passing of the great Reverend Doctor Cecil Douglass Goodwell."

Teary-eyed, emotional and distraught, Deaconess Margaret Fields lowered her head as the Board of Trustees Finance Chairman Paul Howard softly patted her on the back. He then proceeded to say to me, "Pastor Goodwell, you'll have to excuse Sister Margaret for some of the words that she used, but you know she's always meant good and was talking to you from the heart." He then added, "You know I've been one of the biggest supporters of you taking over for your dad here at Mount Caramel Baptist Church. Your dad and I go back a long way and were the best of friends. I was his number one confidante bar none, especially after your mother died of cancer. So what I'm telling you," Trustee Howard cleared his throat, took a deep breath and a sip of bottled water, "is this: what you're doing, Pastor Goodwell, to the music ministry of this church, our associate ministers, and some of our local political friends, is going to destroy this church, our community, and even you, if you keep it up."

While both of their comments were unjustified, I wasn't surprised by their reactions to my recent remarks that the Black church is losing its moral compass and will soon be like the majority of white churches—godless, unrepentant for sin and full of hypocrisy.

But what I said that really had people riled up at the closed-door, ministers-only meeting that somehow made its way to the front page of every newspaper and talk radio show in the city, was that I would not allow for an avowed homosexual State legislator who had recently received his Master of Divinity degree and was a proponent of gay marriage to speak nor preach from the church pulpit despite the fact that he had been instrumental in helping my father acquire both the land and the bond rating that Mount Caramel Baptist Church needed to build the new church community center and its single family housing units.

Even before the latest gossip and grumbling of church members, Mount Caramel was already in an uproar due to my unceremonious removal of the highly popular minister of music, the Reverend Reginald T. Walker, from his leadership post due to his homosexuality.

The political fallout and condemnation from the newly-gentrified community surrounding the church and various other pockets of the church were swift. Overnight, I became the nation's poster child of a homophobic, racist, hate-monger who was ungrateful for all that had been done for him. I was being depicted as a disgrace both to the pulpit and the coalition-building legacy of my father.

I had vowed to God that I would preach His Holy Word in season and out of season, so I wasn't surprised that I was facing the level of opposition that I was dealing with from people who didn't have a genuine relationship with Jesus Christ as Lord and Savior. But it was the weak-minded, pious, no heart, spineless, overly religious sounding, Bible-carrying but not Bible reading, biblical-quoting and misquoting but not biblical-living, hypocritical so-called Christians that filled a large number of seats in the church pews that frustrated me and caused countless sleepless nights and stress.

Every day I reflect on the multiple challenges of leading a congregation in the 21st century that has been seduced and misled by countless charismatic, telegenic, inspirational, motivational charlatans who falsely pose as anointed men and women of God while preaching on a weekly basis a diluted, self-indulgent gospel that is materialistically-driven, biblically-distorted, doctrinally-altered, but nonetheless provides an emotionally intoxicating, uplifting experience and outlet for those who are often truly in need of a positive, healing, encouraging and empowering Christ-centered message.

In the midst of the conversation with Deaconess Margaret Fields and Board of Trustees Finance Chairman Paul Howard, I started to sense that they were waiting for someone else to join us in the church's newly-furbished conference boardroom. The constant looking at their watches and wooden grandfather clock hanging near the entrance of the boardroom door could definitely be construed as evidence that another party was either late to this alleged impromptu meeting or they had unexpectedly finished up before their comrade/co-conspirator's anticipated arrival.

The sudden presence of a sweet fragrance of an expensive, exotic perfume and the repeated refrains of church staff members in the hallway saying, "Wow, that outfit looks nice," "Where did you get them shoes from, girl?" "You always know how to put it together," meant that our surprise guest making her presence known throughout the church building was none other than my beautiful, intelligent, charming and sometimes calculating wife of four years, Vanessa Ford-Goodwell.

Vanessa's curvaceous, statuesque silhouette behind the frosted conference room door was soon revealed when she gracefully opened the door with an equally captivating, glamorous smile, enticing eyes and magnetic presence that made people who came in contact with her feel as though they were around true royalty as well as a genuine person who was concerned about their well-being. No wonder I married her.

"Reverend Goodwell, I hope I'm not interrupting anything," said Vanessa in a soft, demur tone.

Before I could respond back, both Deaconess Margaret and Chairman Howard took the liberty of answering for me in unison, saying, "Come on in. We were just finishing up."

Vanessa looked over at me seeking my concurrence to the invitation she had just heard. With a motion of my head and a hand gesture, I assured Vanessa that I was on one accord with both Margaret and Howard and was totally supportive of her making herself comfortable.

Determined not to let this become an opportunity for the deaconess and trustee chairman to vent before my wife about their opinions of what I was doing wrong in the church, I began to thank them for coming by. Suddenly, they got up from their leather upholstery seats and said, "Thank you for your time, Pastor, and have a wonderfully blessed day."

Once the door had closed completely behind them and the sounds of the deaconess, trustee and others walking or talking in the hallway had become a distant faint muffle, Vanessa, in an inviting, darling-tell-me-all-your-troubles voice, said, "Sweetie, how was your day?"

Not feeling the need to bear my soul to her, nor participate in another therapeutic session with a woman who I could never be certain wanted to hear what was on my mind concerning church issues anyhow, I decided to go with the typical retort, "Fine. How was yours?"

Vanessa, with the skill she had mastered a long time ago, skipped reporting on how her day was and instead chose a different line of questioning that began with, "Is Deaconess Margaret okay? She looked emotionally drained when she left. As the head of the Women's Ministry, is there anything I should know in order to be supportive?"

A gigantic smile consumed my face causing for my cheeks to puff out as I thought to myself, "Oh you're good, Vanessa." Recognizing that my wife was determined to have a conversation on a subject matter that she had obviously already been briefed on, I decided that it was beneficial for both of us if I just acknowledged the fact that she had an agenda and opinion that she wanted to share with me. I then could use this timeframe as an opportunity for me to convey an important Christian ministry message to her.

So I began, "On the Deaconess Fields issue, it shouldn't come as a surprise to you, Vanessa, that Margaret, and in fairness to her several other people in the church, have taken issue with my removal of Reverend Walker as the head of the music ministry."

"David, now that is a classic understatement if I've ever heard one."

"What do you mean?"

"How long did it take for you to come up with that one?" Vanessa checked to make sure that no one was secretly standing outside the room listening in. "David, I have to give it to you. You're always talking about the importance of the church uniting together, but never in my wildest imagination did I think that you could unite Mount Caramel, the Christian right and the progressive left all at the same time, and all against you."

"Vanessa, what are you taking about?"

"What am I talking about?" retorted Vanessa, incredulous. "I'm talking about your ability to pick one of the few issues in the entire Mount Caramel Baptist Church that could unite almost everyone in the church, especially your enemies, to say, 'Pastor, what you did was wrong.' "

"Vanessa, make no mistake about it. I didn't do anything wrong in sitting down Reverend Walker, and to be frank about it, as the pastor of this church and the leader of this congregation, I am about a half step from sitting down almost the whole choir."

"David, don't be ridiculous. You think you have more power than you actually do."

"Vanessa, hear me clearly and make no mistake about it. God has given me all the power and strength I need in order to make the necessary changes to bring this church in line with His Holy Word."

Vanessa paused for what seemed like forever. Visibly frustrated by my lack of appreciation of her concerns, she nonetheless tried her best to maintain a calm, controlled, and dignified voice. "David, this isn't all about you. You are fully aware that I am in a hotly contested primary for the district's state senator seat and need every vote I can get, especially the gay vote. Your homosexual rampage has put me in a very awkward position with key constituent groups that I'm depending on to win this election."

"Vanessa, you may be trying to win votes, but I'm trying to win souls for Christ."

By the expression on her face I could tell she was feeling more and more agitated, so I wasn't surprised when Vanessa sighed and in a very sarcastic manner said, "David, in case you didn't know, Jesus isn't voting in the primaries. The people lined up around this church with protest signs are. So whether you recognize it or not, while this may have once been a predominantly Black district, it no longer is, and even if it was, Black people don't vote like they should, while the homosexual community is very politically active."

"You're not hearing me. I didn't remove Reverend Walker because of my hate for homosexuals; I removed him because of my love for God's Word. The Bible is clear. Homosexuality is a sin, no way around it. As the pastor, and more importantly as a man of God, I could not allow for him as the head of a church ministry to promote a lifestyle that directly conflicts with God's

Word."

"You are such a hypocrite. Why haven't you sat down all the ministers, deacons and Sunday school teachers that are having premarital sex? According to you, fornication is just as much of a sin as homosexuality, so why are you picking on the homosexuals?"

"First of all, Vanessa, it is not according to me but to God's Word. Let's get that straight from the jump. The Bible in Leviticus 18:22, Romans 1:26-27 and a whole lot of other places in both the Old Testament and the New Testament make it perfectly clear that homosexuality is a sin. You can't deny that. You can lie about it. You can make excuses about it. You can say that that was then and this is now. You can come up with whatever rationale or trick of the devil that you want, but you can't change the Word of God."

"David, you still haven't addressed why the focus on homosexuals, and why now, when I'm in the midst of trying to get elected."

"Vanessa, you're right that a lot of issues are affecting our church community, the Black community and people of all races and ethnicities. Homosexuality is just one of them, and I truly recognize that and believe that when I wake up in the morning and look in the mirror, I can be at peace knowing that I have tried my best to bring attention and resources to some of the other major ills that disproportionately affect the Black community, ranging from mis-education, lack of education, homelessness, drug addiction, hunger, poverty, Black on Black crime, unemployment and racism. However, this issue of blatant, unchecked homosexuality in the church has gotten way out of hand and is having a devastating impact on the health of Black women, Black men and

Black families."

"David, you just don't get it. Do you have any idea the amount of backlash that is brewing not only in this church but nationwide? You sat down one of the most popular ministers of music, not only at Mount Caramel but in churches across the country, for being a homosexual. Reverend Walker has been at Mount Caramel for over twenty years. Your dad is the one who hired him. Matter fact, more people know him and come to church every Sunday to hear him sing than to hear you preach."

"You may be right about who they're coming to see...."

"There ain't no might in it," shot back Vanessa.

"Okay, okay, okay. I get the point that Reverend Walker is very popular and liked by a whole lot of people, but that doesn't change the fact that homosexuality is a sin."

I could tell by the way she was looking at me that Vanessa falsely sensed that she had made a major breakthrough with me and forwarding her position. She made eye contact with me, and then gestured for affect to the cross displayed on the right-hand side of the conference room. She turned back towards me and said, "Doesn't God love everybody, and if so, doesn't everybody include homosexuals?"

"I never ever said that God doesn't love everybody. But don't get it twisted, Vanessa. God loving us doesn't mean that our actions are always pleasing to God. If a person decides that for whatever reason they are unwilling to change from their sinful ways and accept Jesus Christ as Lord and Savior, then they will go to Hell. No question about it."

"What does this have to do with Reverenced Walker? He proclaims Jesus Christ as Lord and Savior." Vanessa was now annoyed.

"That is exactly my point. I sat him down as head of the music ministry not because he committed a singular homosexual act or repeated homosexual acts. I removed him from church leadership because he defines himself by the sin. Nobody is sinless, but every day we need to try to sin less. The entire church is full of people, including myself, who have fallen short of God's standard and have committed sin. But the difference for myself and many others is that we ask for forgiveness from God for our sin when we unfortunately fall to temptation. Reverend Walker has not only committed the homosexual act of sin, but he now defines himself by that sin. No other sinner does that. Reverend Walker is totally unrepentant."

"Are you saying that he can't be a member of this church because he is a homosexual?"

"Not at all. What I'm saying is that as a church leader and as a Christian in general, you may struggle with sin because we are all human, but what can never be acceptable for any Christian is to stop struggling and fighting against sin with the power given to us by God. We cannot claim the sin. When you get down to it, that is my number one problem with Reverend Walker. He took it to the next level. If he were to acknowledge that homosexuality is a sin and was having difficulty with fighting the temptation, I never would have sat him down from church leadership. But I cannot allow him to promote sin from the pulpit or any other leadership role in our church."

"Let's move Reverend Walker out of this for a second and look at what you are doing to me as your wife," maneuvered Vanessa, choosing another approach. I knew her goal was to get me to publicly apologize for my recent comments.

"I don't see the correlation between my releasing Reverend Walker from his ministerial duties and our marriage."

"That's your problem right there, David. You are so damn selfish. You know I'm in the midst of a major political fight to win the party nomination. You should have at least had the decency to talk with me beforehand so we could discuss if this was the right thing to do. But without consulting me, you go out and make this major decision that has consequences not only for you, but for me."

"I'm the pastor, not you and not us, but me and me alone," I shouted back.

"How dare you. After all of the sacrifices I've made as your wife, you come at me with some 'I'm the pastor.' You have truly lost your mind. You may be the pastor to them," Vanessa pointed angrily towards the window facing the church parking lot, "but to me, you are my husband, and don't forget it."

"What is that supposed to mean?"

"It means that when I walked down the aisle and married you there was no talk about you being a minister or a pastor. It was all about us building an empire and a future together. Just you and me against the world. The man I fell in love with was a brilliant man who had a promising future and who respected the fact that I was an intelligent, independent business woman who had her own flavor. I never once wanted to be a pastor's wife, first lady or any other title in a church." Vanessa the politician/actress was starting to come out as she pressed on in making her point in such a dramatic way. Even I didn't believe she would wrap up her comments with, "I loved you enough, David, to leave my family mem-

S. James Guitard

bers, friends and even the small business that I had labored years in building in order for us to move back to your parents' hometown. You know for a fact that I didn't initially want to come here, but I loved you so much that I sacrificed my dreams for you. So what I am asking from you now is for you to sacrifice for me for a change."

From across the boardroom table, I began a slow, but continually faster and louder sequence of thunderous applause to express my appreciation for the wonderful performance my wife had just put on. "Don't for one minute try to play on my emotions. You know damn well you didn't come here for me, and I'm not even mad at you for that. I'm just glad that in the end you decided to come. But you would be doing yourself a major disservice and fooling yourself if you didn't think that I knew you were contemplating getting a divorce from me until my father promised you that he could arrange for you to win the newly redrawn state senator seat."

"No disrespect to your deceased father, but if he or anyone else told you that, then they are a liar."

"No need for you to go there, Vanessa. I already told you, I'm not mad at you for it, so there is no reason for you to lie."

"You want talk about lies, huh? How about you never told me that you and Crystal used to date before we met? How about I had to read in the newspaper today allegations that Shelton Calloway, the accused murderer staying at our house, may be your son? How about you telling me in the middle of the night when I'm dead asleep that you may need to lend some family member some money, but you never say that it's bail money for your illegitimate son? Do I need to continue?"

72

Vanessa had hit a very sensitive nerve that I had yet to acknowledge. I never intentionally planned to lie to her about Crystal and me having an intimate relationship. I just never spoke about it because it was such a long time ago. I didn't see the need to bring up a past relationship that existed before we got married and I was years removed away from. In regards to Shelton, I was not going to disown a child who is seeking adult guidance during a difficult period in his life, especially when my wife and I can't have kids and he is like the kid I never had. But that's all he is. Shelton and I may have some things in common—our love for basketball, both of us have been star athletes in high school—but despite all of what we share in family looks, interests and his desire to have a strong masculine male figure in his life, I am not his father. And I have undisputable private paternity test results to prove it. But at the same time, if Shelton thinking I might possibly be his father makes it easier for him to talk to me and listen to the valuable advice that I can share with him which could redirect him in the right direction, then so be it. The bigger issue is not that Shelton isn't my child, but that Shelton isn't my brother's either, and he doesn't know it.

CHAPTER TEN

Either you take that butcher knife off the dining room table and slit your baby's throat, or I'll shoot your mother dead in the head," threatened a menacing, masked gunman appearing out of the shadows to a semiconscious Prince Murda.

The severity of enduring over an hour-long, blood-splattering pistol whipping had swelled tight Prince Murda's outer eyelids so badly that he could barely make out the distorted image of his weeping mother kneeling before a completely deranged crazy man. Despite her constant heart-filled pleas for mercy or compassion, the armed man remained completely unmoved and unsympathetic to her tears and desires to live.

"Prince, I'm gonna give you less than thirty seconds to kill your daughter, but if you don't want to, then don't worry. I'm going to enjoy watching the expression on your face when I pull this trigger and blow your mom's brain out."

Badly beaten, slightly delusional and squinting constantly from the throbbing pain emanating from a possibly fractured left rib, a courageous Prince Murda sat lurched over at the dining room table trying his best to quickly regain his composure after having been knocked lifeless by a man hiding behind the front door of his mother's darkened apartment.

An innocent, curly-haired, two-year-old baby girl slept silently still in her car seat atop the dining room table while a razor sharp stainless steal knife laid just as motionless.

Sensing precious time slipping away from him and justifiably boiling with hatred, deep-seated anger and intense rage, Prince Murda fought internally to channel his thoughts into a constructive, well-thought-out, heroic plan to save his mother and daughter from what looked like an imminent grizzly death. No amount of money, no matter what the financial cost was or price he had to pay with his own life, was beyond promising if it would allow for his loved ones to walk out of this experience alive.

"I'm begging you, please don't do this, man. Please, please, please. I'll give you whatever you want. No matter what it is, I'll get it. Money. Drugs. Whatever. I'm just saying, please don't kill my baby or my mother," pleaded Prince Murda as he calculated with the mindset of a military general the different scenarios and options that might be available to him to possibly distract the gunman just enough so that he could tackle the shooter before a gunshot ripped through his mother's temple.

The Sig Sauer P229, Black 9mm handgun with laser scope looked eerily similar to the type of weapon Prince Murda had used in countless armed robberies, shootouts with rival drug gangs and for protection while selling different kinds of narcotics out of a rundown subsidized housing unit. The sight of seeing the loaded, black, steel barrel of death pressed against his mother's forehead versus discretely tucked in the front of his jeans and covered by a popular sports jersey was humbling.

Prince Murda understood that he needed to figure out quickly who and why this lunatic was about to kill the one person who regardless of how much dirt he had done on the street always said,

"No matter what, you're still my baby." Why would someone be so sick and desiring of revenge that they would want me to kill an innocent child that hadn't done anything wrong? Recognizing that his time was almost up and he needed to make a decision, Prince Murda, with tears streaming from his eyes, reached out across the dining room table, squeezed the handle of the butcher knife, lifted the blade into the air and stared at the reflection of his battle-scarred, saddened face.

It wasn't supposed to be this way. After surviving countless gang assassination attempts, bad drug deals, police stings, jealous haters, stints in juvenile detention centers, baby mamma drama, petty beefs and endless nights of hustling on the block corner, Prince Murda had found a level of peace several years later through selling mix tapes, doing street promotions for local urban artists and making hip-hop collaborations with different people he knew from his childhood.

According to the news accounts, street gossip and mix tapes played throughout the city, Prince "Murda" Hall had established himself as a Pure Hustler who Pimps Hoes, Packs Heat and would "Murda" anyone who thought they could compete with him lyrically. Up until very recently, the only actual murdering Prince Hall had ever done was during freestyle competitions and on promotional demos.

If you had seen the smiling, eager-to-learn, knapsack-toting Prince Hall in first grade, you never would have thought that this adorable young boy who had a fascination with music, computers and any type of electronic gadgets would later be the focus of a television news flash and extensive police manhunt for the slaying of several people at a popular nightclub, including an honor

77

student who happened to be at the wrong place at the wrong time.

In contrast, Prince Hall's older twin brothers were serving consecutive life sentences for drug distribution and murder. The infamous older Hall brothers had run an elaborate drug cartel built upon intimidation, top-of-the-line drug products and a total disregard for human life. The Halls' mother in her early youth was an up-and-coming R&B singer who had developed a cocaine drug habit that eventually led to crack addiction. After her money got tight, her man left her. The boys, without an extended family to care for them, were left to fend for themselves and took to a life on the streets.

The Hall brothers' petulance to sharing a large part of the drug profits with their crew created an artificial loyalty and mystique. Omar and Kevin's usage and celebration of violence as a means to an end made crossing the Hall family a life and death situation.

Omar was a gifted basketball and playground legend who, despite his enormous basketball talents, was unable to qualify academically to go to college.

Major universities as well as community colleges were still trying to find a way to make him eligible to play, when Omar's name surfaced mistakenly in a murder investigation concerning the gang-style assassination of a notorious drug dealer named Teflon. Omar's twin brother Kevin had several outstanding warrants, so when he was rounded up by the police as part of a neighborhood get-tough-on-crime sweep, Kevin pretended that he was Omar in order to avoid arrest. When the police connected Kevin to Teflon's killing, they mistakenly released a photo with Omar's name all across the city. While Omar was eventually cleared, the negative publicity, his poor academic grades and the family's connection to the drug game were too much for any school, university or NBA team to risk.

Omar initially resisted being in the drug game, but constantly being mistaken for his older brother had placed his life in jeopardy on many occasions. He eventually started carrying a 9mm barreta automatic gun for protection. Omar had assumed a lot of the risk associated with the drug game but never received any of the money. After years of seeing Kevin flourish in the drug game, driving expensive cars, having flashy clothes, gorgeous women and pockets full of money, Omar finally caved in when Kevin informed him that there was a murder hit on their younger sister Theresa Hall for having turned state's evidence against a drug supplier on the other side of town. The only way their sister would live was if the drug supplier and the drug case went away, which could only occur if the dealer and his drug posse were dead.

Kevin wouldn't be able to kill everybody himself; he needed help, and the only person he knew he could trust was none other than Omar.

As far as Omar was concerned, there really wasn't much to think about. His sister was going to get killed by drug dealers if he didn't help. His brother Kevin was going to die trying to stop their sister from getting killed, and it didn't take a genius to figure out that whoever would be responsible for the death of Theresa and his brother Kevin would eventually kill him and their baby brother, Prince Hall, in order to avoid any retaliation from the family. The only choice, or so Omar thought, was to join Kevin and kill everyone who they thought was a threat, and with that, the city's murder rate shot up to a five-year high within two weeks.

Federal, state and local officials joined together in order to establish a special task force to investigate the sudden rash of murders that was destroying years of undercover police work. The older Hall brothers, while not found guilty for murder nor drug possession, were found guilty a year and a half later of conspiracy to import cocaine, conspiracy to possess with intent to distribute cocaine and conspiracy to launder money.

Prince Hall was smart enough to recognize that the high visibility that came from his brothers' extensively covered trial and conviction, mandatory drug sentencing laws, new wiretapping legislation, election year politics, plea deals by snitching, convicted felons and the alphabet cops (FBI, DEA, DHS and DOJ) with big dossiers on the Hall family name, meant that any effort to pick up where his brothers left off would definitely result in a conviction and life sentence for himself.

Stressed out and needing a different type of hustle, Prince Murda decided to go to a popular out-of-town strip club in order to unwind, relax, look at sexy women and think of a strategy to get paid. In between a couple of strippers' sets, ordering drinks and loading up on some dollar bills, some fives and tens, Prince Murda reclined back in a leather comforter located to the side of the stage and received the surprise of the night when the woman sliding down the stripper's pole with the nickname Mo' Chocolate was none other than his sister Theresa.

Embarrassed and now more stressed out than when he first arrived at the G-spot Strip Club, Prince Murda stormed the fluorescent-lit stage, grabbed his sister by the arm and dragged her in the direction of the dressing room door. From every direction, grimacing muscle-bound bouncers started charging him with miniature baseball bats and steel pipes.

Having left his favorite gun under the front seat of his SUV parked outside, Prince Murda eluded the first bouncer who tried to swing at him, threw a chair at another and then hopped over the bar counter, broke a champagne bottle and held the jagged edge of broken glass up against the throat of the female bartender. He then motioned for everyone, including a few G-spot customers who had tried to subdue him, to back up or he would cut the woman's throat.

Theresa, to her credit, was earnestly pushing her way through the crowd while intermittently screaming, "Don't hurt him. Don't hurt him. We're cool. We're cool." By the time she emerged at the front of the mob, Prince Murda had tightened his yoke around the bartender's neck with a death grip similar to the ones used in ultimate wrestling fighting tournaments. Prince Murda's I-will-definitely-cut-her-throat-wide-open scowl was teamed up with a you-better-not-try-me icy stare.

A deep, rich baritone voice that commanded respect and got it, told everybody, "Back up and relax. I got this." Without hesitation or conflict, the bouncers and some stray customers started moving away from the bar and made a path for the immaculately dressed, medium-build man with a tattoo on the left-hand side of his neck.

Theresa's pleas of, "Please don't hurt him. Please, please, please. He's my younger brother, and he didn't know I worked here. I promise you, I will make it up to you. Just let him go," were then followed by turning to Prince Hall and saying, "Prince, listen to me. You don't want to do this. Let the woman go."

The determining factor in Prince Murda leaving the G-spot

Strip Club alive was not Theresa's half-naked groveling nor the danger he posed to the expendable female bartender. It was the fact that at the time of his Prince's outburst, the club owner had been engaged in intense discussions with another man from an independent music label about their joint desperate need to find a legitimate way to hide the money they made from drug profits. While he was still chillin' in the recliner, the music producer had recognized Prince Murda as the winner of several local MC-battle contests and as the younger brother of the infamous, imprisoned Hall Brothers. Prior to the ruckus, they were planning to arrange for one of their representatives to approach Prince Murda about signing on to their label.

So instead of Prince Murda's body being mutilated, decomposed in acid and later dumped in an abandoned field for disrespecting the mob run and owned G-spot Strip Club establishment, his apology was accepted, and he left the club with a record label contract, $10,000 in cash, and a promise that his sister could stop stripping and her college tuition would be paid. With an appointment to pick up a brand-new leased fully-equipped convertible with rims, an upcoming meeting with one of the top music beat producers, and future videos being produced by industry powerhouse Calloway Enterprises, Prince Murda felt that he was on top of the world.

Several underground and commercial hit songs later, guest appearances on other hip-hop and R&B artist albums, Prince Murda's popularity both within the United States and across the globe continued to expand. The number of magazine covers he appeared on multiplied; the sold-out concerts quadrupled; the video requests on cable were endless, and the groupies were infinite.

Everything, including the enormous level of love and hate from people he knew and didn't know inside and outside of the industry was increasing. The only thing not growing was the money he was bringing in. Actually, Prince Murda was being exploited so badly by Pure Hustla Records that despite the outward appearances of fancy cars, designer clothes, wads of spending money and jewelry, the majority of everything else that people associated with him was actually owned by the record company or were only stage props to promote the videos.

Determined to get out of the monstrosity of a music contract that had him owing Pure Hustla Records hundreds of thousands of dollars despite the fact that he made the company tens of millions of dollars, Prince Murda requested on numerous occasions to renegotiate his contract. When that failed, he threatened to leave, and when that didn't work, Prince Murda hired an attorney and requested for an audit of Pure Hustla Records, Pure Hustla Entertainment and all entities associated with the music, apparel, or other enterprises capitalizing off of Prince Murda Hall.

"I don't know who you are, but I'm begging you. Please in the name of God let my mother and daughter go," Prince Murda desperately pleaded as thirty seconds had just transpired.

From out of the shadows, another ominous figure materialized in his mother's dining room. The sight of the man let Prince Murda know that this wasn't about some street jealousy or old neighborhood feud that had come back to haunt him. His recent desperate attempt to get out his contract through the use of blackmail had backfired.

"You do know who I am." Prince Murda recognized the popular pastor's voice right away.

Certain that his mother was going to die since he was too far away to get to the armed gunman before the gun would go off, Prince Murda mustered his remaining strength and lunged with the butcher knife at the minister that had just entered the room.

An intense struggle ensued. Screams for help went unheeded. Blood trickled to the floor. Bullets sliced the air. Dead bodies crumbled. Police sirens blared. The apartment door frantically slammed closed, and a two-year-old baby girl screamed at the top of her lungs from her car seat. Alone and alive.

CHAPTER ELEVEN

E verybody has skeletons, no matter who they are. I don't care if the district attorney's skeletons are buried 100 feet deep in an airtight, sealed casket surrounded by cement reinforced steel walls. I want them found, dug up and exposed on every news program and gossip blog in the country."

"Crystal, calm down. You're talking about the district attorney. You just can't go scandalizing the DA. There is a lot at stake."

"I know that. But nobody, and I mean nobody, is going to use my son as political capital so they can win a congressional seat."

"You bear some of the responsibility. With all the millions of dollars we have on the table connected to the Mount Caramel Baptist Church neighborhood revitalization project, you had no business allowing your son to become a rapper with the name Killa C just so he could end up in a rap war between him and Prince Murda."

"In retrospect, maybe you're right, Trustee Howard. But at the time it just seemed like easy money. Shelton wanted desperately to get in the music industry. Everywhere you turn people are making money off of his athletic ability due to his amateur status. The only person not making money off of Shelton is Shelton and our family."

"So you decided to pimp your son."

"No. I didn't decide to pimp my son. Shelton is almost an adult and there were a lot of music companies coming out of the wood work offering him deals. How stupid would it have been to forgo all the hundreds of thousands of dollars that were going to be made off Shelton's rap career when our family owns an entertainment enterprise? Plus, who better than my husband and I to ensure that he doesn't get exploited by one of our competitors?"

Trustee Howard glared at me, shrugged his shoulders and then leaned as far back as the vibrating massage chair could take him before proceeding to say, "Crystal, you're not mentioning the real reason."

"You want me to say that we need money? Well, damn it, everybody needs money, including the Calloways."

"That may be, but your son is now charged with the highly-publicized killing of Evelyn James. Gossip magazines, talk radio programs and sleazy television shows can't get enough of a story that has adultery and an unsolved murder of a beautiful runway model and popular video vixen who was secretly dating two rap artists in the middle of a hip-hop war."

Feeling a motherly urge to protect my son from the unfounded media smear campaign that was being developed by the politically aspiring district attorney, I shot back at Trustee Howard with a thundering, "My son is innocent."

"You're not getting this, Crystal. It is not about whether or not Shelton is innocent. It's about the fact that there are millions of dollars on the line connected to the neighborhood re-gentrification initiative and the upcoming presidential election. The powerful players in this game are not concerned with your son's innocence or guilt. That is your issue and your issue only. Just don't do anything to impact the deals that are in motion."

"And what if I do? What are you going to do to me? Kill me? I'm not the Reverend Cecil Douglass Goodwell."

"What did you say?"

"You heard me, Trustee Howard. I'm not DJ's father. I don't believe, not for one second, that Reverend Goodwell's car went speeding off a cliff and burst into flames because he had a sudden heart attack. You and the people you represent had a role in that. I know you did, whether you admit it or not."

"Crystal, stand still and don't move, not one inch."

Startled by how fast the conversation between the deacon and I had deteriorated into a hostile situation, I stared in total disbelief and shock when he removed a concealed shiny black object from his right hand coat pocket. Not knowing what his intentions were and feeling that my options were limited, all I could muster up to say was, "I can't believe that you are pulling a gun out on me."

"Don't say a word, and I mean it. Just slowly pass me your blazer and then begin taking off your blouse."

"Paul, I know that you don't think I'm wearing a wire."

"This is your last warning, Crystal. I don't want to hear anything from you. Just take off your clothes and place them right there on the chair. If I'm wrong, I deeply apologize and you can go out and buy yourself something nice and bill it to me, but if you are wearing a wire, I'm going to shoot more bullets into you than you shot into Evelyn James."

"What are you talking about? I didn't kill Evelyn."

"Forget the lies, Crystal. Just keep taking off your clothes. Drawers included."

Defiantly I stood in the middle of the room with my hands placed on my hips and let Trustee Howard know in no uncertain terms that I was not going tolerate this type of blatant disrespect from him or anybody else. There was no way he could have known about my killing Evelyn. He obviously was testing me to see how I would respond. I know for a fact that when I left the hotel that night there wasn't a single soul outside the hotel. So if he wanted to get his jolly off of seeing me naked, he would have to settle like everybody else for that bootleg video circulating on the web that showed me having sex with several men in college. The video from yesteryear was the result of me being drugged at a party. I could not believe for the life of me that he actually thought I had on a wire, so I yelled at the top of my lungs, "I'm not taking off my underwear for nobody."

"You can take them off alive or I can take them off you dead, but they're coming off regardless. Now hurry the hell up."

"You have got to be kidding."

"Crystal, unless you are butt naked in the next few seconds, the next words that will be coming from your mouth will be 'Jesus, help me' while you're bleeding to death. Now give me everything. Bra. Drawers. Jewlery. Everything. This is my very last warning."

Uncertain of whether Trustee Howard had the balls to shoot me or not, I reluctantly concluded that it was not only advantageous for me to take off all my clothes, but it was to my benefit to give the Board of Trustees Finance Chairman a sensual impromptu striptease that would raise more than his blood pressure. While his mind is spent fantasying what would it be like to be with me sexually, I could focus on a plan to deal with my scariest nightmare coming true. Somebody knew that I had killed Evelyn

James.

"Now that's what I'm talking about, Crystal. I didn't know you had it in you, girl. I'm impressed."

"There. Are you happy now? Everything is off. No need to point a gun at me."

Trustee Howard began sifting through my clothes for electronic devices. "Crystal, just be happy you're not wearing a wire. Your sick mother has already endured enough grief and embarrassment of late. You don't want to turn up dead and have your mother find out you've been framing her grandson for a murder that you committed, do you?"

"I don't know where you are getting these lies from, but I didn't have anything to do with Evelyn's death, and I am insulted that you would think that I would risk my own child's life just to avoid admitting to the self-defense killing of that despicable woman."

"So, you are going for the self-defense angle, huh? How would you know that she was killed in an act of self-defense if you weren't there and your son didn't kill her? Leave it alone, Crystal. I'm not police, and I don't care that you killed her. I know with your law degree you think you have it going on, but do you really think that you are that clever that you could have murdered someone and not left any DNA evidence or clues?" Pausing for effect, Trustee Howard then said, "If the people who are connected to this regentrification project and the upcoming presidential election did not think that you were more valuable alive than dead because of the influence that you have over your ex-lover, Pastor Goodwell, then you wouldn't even be here talking to me."

"You can think whatever you want. It makes no difference to me. I didn't do anything, and there is no evidence to suggest otherwise," I replied while putting back on my panties and straightening out my bra.

"Save it for a jury. As far as I'm concerned, Crystal, you stick to your lies all you want, but let me tell you something you didn't know. You killed an FBI agent who was under cover. Evelyn was in the process of trying to help the FBI acquire money laundering or drug conspiracy charges against Calloway Enterprises and made the stupid mistake of falling in love with your son, Shelton."

"Paul, what are you talking about? Calloway Enterprises doesn't have anything to do with money laundering or drugs. The district attorney is just using the celebrity status of my family name to get news for his congressional race. The charges against me and my son are all lies."

"For once you are telling the truth. The district attorney's office, under the advisement of the FBI, placed charges against you not because you are guilty, but to place pressure on your husband who definitely is involved in money laundering, drugs and a whole lot more."

"Everything you are saying about Steven and Evelyn is a lie, and I don't believe it."

"Crystal, I got to admit, I was pretty surprised to see the surveillance video of you going into the motel shortly after your husband left. The business partners I represent are powerful and wealthy people with deep political connections. We had Evelyn James under our surveillance for quite a while. Your killing her surprised everybody."

Startled by the candor with which the trustee expressed no sorrow for the killing of an FBI agent and fellow parishioner, my facial expressions were torn between astonishment, fear, admiration and disbelief.

"Don't look at me that way. I see what you're thinking, Crystal. You think you confirmed that the motel didn't have any surveillance cameras so I must be lying about seeing you there. Well, you should have paid attention to the minivan across the street from the motel, because we have dated video footage that puts you at the scene of the killing. The only question that I don't have an answer for is, why did you kill her?"

"I don't have anything more to say."

"Well, I do. So I tell you what. Effective immediately, you are to cease and desist any plans you have to scandalize or negatively impact the campaign or future election of the district attorney to Congress. His winning or losing the congressional seat could change which party controls Congress. In addition, as previously agreed upon, you will keep quiet about certain private matters concerning the deceased Reverend Cecil Goodwell, the regentrification plans for the neighborhood as well as the plan to use certain prominent Black preachers to suppress or confuse the Black voters in the upcoming presidential election. In exchange, you will not only get the money originally promised to you, but I will arrange for an extra $75,000 to be given to you as an advance to hire the best damn attorney you can find to get your son off for murder on a technicality, as long as you promise to not comprise the deals already on the table and work with us to string the case on through the election."

"And if I don't?"

"Well, Crystal, all I can tell you is as a trustee of Mount Caramel Baptist Church, I pray it doesn't come to that, but if it does, then I will miss you dearly as well as your mother, too.

Because the moment you betray me, the Preachers' Syndicate and the people I represent, then next time we cross paths you, your son, your mother and you will have been beaten to death so unmercifully that a closed casket will seem too open. So I tell you what, why don't you get fully dressed, take this couple of thousands that I'm giving you today, get a good night's rest, and I will see you bright and early tomorrow morning at church."

CHAPTER TWELVE

They Talk by Faith but They Walk by Doubt," were the words God had given me to preach. My prayers had once again been answered and just in the nick of time. During the last several nights, the weight of all the political fallout and controversy surrounding me was starting to have an effect. The endless gossip, second-guessing, backstabbing, ulterior motives, fake smiles, and outright lies were starting to wear me down. And that was just the people in my congregation.

When you add never-ending, scandal-driven news coverage concerning the murder of parishioner Evelyn James, the arrest of my favorite nephew Shelton Calloway as her killer, the revelation for me that not only is my marriage falling apart, but my wife considers me a political liability to her election aspirations, then you may be able to understand why at times I've had yearnings for the days when the words "reverend" and "pastor" were not associated with the name David Josiah Goodwell.

As a man of God who is authentically called to preach the gospel of Jesus Christ with truth and power, God revealed to me what may be one of the most life-altering understandings of my relationship with God as a Christian attempting to live a Heaven-bound life in a Hell-bent world. God said I could make a choice to go backwards, but I couldn't go back, because it doesn't exist anymore. My eyes had been opened up to sin, the truth of Jesus Christ as Lord and Savior, the conviction of the Holy Spirit as well as the blessings and protections that come from a relationship with Him.

So as I stood before the congregation, I said, "Those of you who are physically able throughout the church, could you join me as we stand upon our feet and reverence the Word of God. Lord, we thank You and praise You for this moment. With all the hardships, heartbreaks and hurts of life that we have experienced and are in some cases going through right now, we come before You, God, because we know that You are a healer, liberator, Savior and redeemer. We are in need of Your guidance right now, Lord. Many of us this day, when we are honest with ourselves, recognize that we are struggling not only in finances but in faith. But we know, God, that You know our hearts and our hurts, whether they be concerning our relationships with family, friends, significant others, careers, the world or ourselves.

"We also know, Lord, that You know where we've traveled and the roads we have taken to get there, and that is why more than ever we need You to order our steps. You said that You have magnified Your Holy Word above all Your name, so God, many of us join together in prayer and fellowship today so that we may be empowered, strengthened, healed, encouraged, and renewed in all facets of our lives by Your Holy Word.

"Individually and collectively, Lord, we say thank You, God, for Your love, Your mercy, Your grace, Your patience, kindness, forgiveness and redemption. In all that we are and all that You do, we praise You, God. May the words of our mouth and the meditation of our hearts be pleasing in Your sight, O Lord, our strength and our redeemer, Amen.

"You may be all seated. In the few moments that are ours together, I would like, with your prayers, to converse with you from the heart about talking by faith but walking by doubt. If you have a Bible, turn to the book of Mark, chapter 8, verses 22-25. The Word of God says: 'Then He came to Bethsaida; and they brought a blind man to Him, and begged Him to touch him. So He took the blind man by the hand and led him out of the town. And when He had spit on his eyes and put His hands on him, He asked him if he saw anything. And he looked up and said, "I see men like trees, walking." Then He put His hands on his eyes again and made him look up. And he was restored and saw everyone clearly.' You may be seated.

"I share this text with you for many reasons. As many of you know, the storms of turmoil and confusion have been battering this congregation as well as me as your pastor and brother in Christ. The winds of false allegations, purposeful distortions and blatant lies have been whipped into a frenzy by instigators and provocateurs in the press, our surrounding church community, special interest groups with various agendas and unfortunately even members of our beloved Mount Caramel Baptist Church.

"I'm going to be very candid and open with you. When I woke up this morning and turned on the morning news and saw talk show pundits masquerading as journalists calling me everything but a man of God, I was disheartened. When I flipped to another television station and watched false reports about me having had an affair with parishioner Evelyn James as well as reports by alleged confidential sources that I may have had a role in her death, I became further saddened. When commentators shared false accusations back and forth that not only had I committed adultery against my wife but I fathered a child that is now being charged with the murder of Ms. James, and to top that off, the woman I am falsely being accused of having the affair with is my brother's wife, I became more despondent.

"Those of you who haven't grown up in this church don't know that Steven Calloway is my brother, and the reality is there was no reason for you to know, but let's just keep everything out on the table. No affair occurred between my sister-in-law Crystal and me, and no, I'm not sleeping with my brother's wife. I'm not hiding nothing. I'm going to tell the truth and shame the devil with every breath I breathe and every word and action I live.

"The personal character assassinations against me have been ruthless, unending and painful. I've been blindsided not only by the unwillingness of many church leaders to speak truth to power but their unwillingness to speak the powerful truth about the Word of God. In a conversation I had yesterday with Deaconess Brown and Deacon Johnson at a local community center, what stood out to me the most in the midst of their asking me how was I holding up under all the pressure and drama was the fact that they were glad that I had a personal relationship with Jesus Christ.

"Many of you may think that it is automatic for me to have a personal relationship with God because my father was a renowned pastor and I spent the majority of my early life growing up in the church, but what I've come to understand is that there is a difference between being in church and Christ being in you. Growing up in church and attending church every Sunday may make you know of God, but it doesn't mean that you know God. Matter fact, many churches, including, quiet as it's kept our own

Mount Caramel Baptist Church, are full of people who attend or are a member of a church but have never become disciples of Christ. And don't for a moment think that it is just the people in the pews who don't have a personal relationship with Jesus Christ as Lord and Savior. When we are honest with ourselves, we will acknowledge the fact that churches all across this country are full of choir members who can sing a hymn but don't actually know Him.

"During yesterday, I left the local community center after talking with Deaconess Brown and Deacon Johnson being thankful to them for introducing me to Jesus Christ in a way that I could understand when I was a young man. But most of all, I was grateful for the Christian examples that they provided in standing up against injustice, fighting for what was right with the power of God and refusing to live in a church bubble that was disengaged from the political, social and economic oppression that occurs in our community as well as the world at-large.

"What I did not leave the community center with, unfortunately, despite my happiness of knowing that I had a relationship with Jesus Christ, was any closer understanding of my ability to see how I was going to make it out of the turmoil I find myself in. It may be shocking for those of you who have a relationship with Jesus and those of you who don't that there are times when I can't see how I'm going to make it. This is from a man who knows based upon my past that God would not have brought me this far to leave me now. I know for a fact that God has brought me a mighty long way and has blessed me and protected me from many a danger. But when I think of the challenges, obstacles, difficulties of life and hell that I have been catching of late from both in the world and even church members, I have a greater level of understanding of the man in the book of Mark, chapter 9, verse 24, when he shouted to God with tears in his eyes, 'Lord I believe, but help me with my disbelief.'

"I thought you, too, would understand as I do what it is like for the blind man in the book of Mark, chapter 8, verses 22-23 to not only be exposed to God, but to be touched by God and even be led by God, and despite all of that, he still can't see where he is going. This is some real honest talk we are having right here. Do you know, as I know, what it is like to know God, accept God as Lord and Savior, be touched and filled by the awesome power of God, and on top of that not only have your hand but your life in Jesus', walking with God and still can't see your way out of the level of pain, persecution and problems that you are dealing with?

"Do you know what it is like to be a believer in Jesus Christ and still, when you are honest with yourself, you have to admit that you can't see a single bit how you are going to make it financially, emotionally or professionally? Your bills got bills. Money is tight, and you just can't see how you're going to make it?

"Professionally, the job market looks bleak. You want to move up the ladder, but the only thing that is moving up is the unemployment figures and the stress you feel in a dead-end job. Emotionally you are stressed out, burned out, tired and weary. This much is true, you know you are saved and walking with Jesus, and it is because of that, if you are honest with yourself as I have been, that you start to have some questions for God. That's right. Don't look at me strange. I know what it is like to have some questions for God. I woke up this morning with all the hell that I'm facing with some questions for God.

" 'Cause if the truth be told, if it was up to me, I would have been blessed to see my way out of my circumstances a long time ago. It's not like Jesus isn't in the healing business. When Jesus touched the blind man in and led the blind man out of the town, God could have if God chose to, healed the blind man right on the spot, but instead, God led the blind man who he had touched, blindly.

"And so it is sometimes with you and I. God has touched us. God is leading us, but we are often still blind to how we're going to make it out of the drama that we're in. It would be one thing if God couldn't make it so we could see our way out of the struggle that we're facing, but it is totally another thing to have to grasp the reality that God has chosen at this time in our life to leave us in a blind state while at the same time God is desiring us to hold on to Him and follow Him blindly to wherever God is taking us.

"Part of my ability to have some level of peace in the midst of my storms is knowing that while I can't see my way out, I know I'm connected and have not only had my hand but my life in God, who is in the miracle business. Before you get to chapter 8 in the book of Mark and the blind man in city of Bethsaida, Jesus has already healed Peter's mother-in-law of sickness, the leper of leprosy, the paralyzed man who couldn't walk, the man with the withered hand, the woman with the issue of blood, Jairus's daughter from death and the man who was deaf.

"So if you are in the sound of my voice and you ain't deaf like the man Jesus healed and you know for yourself that Jesus is a healer, then what I want for you to do right now is tap your neighbor next to you, and if you don't have one, don't worry about it, just stand up on your feet and shout, 'Jesus is a healer.'

"Now that we have collectively established for everyone around us that we know for a fact that Jesus Christ is a bona fide healer, I want to draw your attention to the fact that some of the people in this congregation who are staring at you right now aren't rejoicing with us or shouting for joy with us. Instead, they are laughing at us, mocking us, talking trash about us, because they may know about the fact that you got some issues and circumstances in your life where you can't see where you going. And they want to know, where is your God?

"Well, I'm getting ready to go, but before I leave, I want to answer that for you and for me. With all the drama going on around me, I may not have sight, but I have gained some insight about God and what God is teaching me and you as well as what He is allowing our temporary blindness to teach others.

"Lesson one. God is separating us from those who talk by faith but walk by doubt, or in some cases, don't walk with God at all. Everybody who is in the sound of my voice, I want you to know that I may not be able to see where I am going, but I know I'm walking with Jesus, and He not only sees it all, He knows it all, and He can do it all. So as long as I walk with Jesus and keep my hand in Jesus' hand, then I will be able to handle it. You don't hear me. If you got your hand in Jesus' hand, then you can handle it.

"Lesson two. The questions you have to ask yourself are, are you willing to follow Jesus when you don't know where He is going to take you, and if you aren't being led by God, then what is leading you in the midst of your darkness? 'Cause I've learned over time that you got to make sure it is Jesus who is leading you. Not your girlfriend. Not your boyfriend. Not your spouse. Not your pastor, but Jesus. Different people may be instrumental in your life in leading you to Jesus, but ultimately you need to make sure that you are following Jesus. In life as your pastor, I may serve as the jumper cable of life connecting you initially to the power of Jesus, but when all is said and done, there is no power in the jumper cable except for when it is connected to the power source. You need to make sure that your faith and your belief are not placed in the jumper cable but in the power that can only come from God.

"Lesson three. Just as the blind man in Mark, chapter 8, verses 22-23, the place of your blindness and the place of your healing may be different places, and because of that, you have to be willing sometimes to accept change and moving on in order that you can get to the place where you can truly see. You have to be willing to make moves while at the same time make sure that in your desire to follow God that you don't get ahead of God and what God wants to do in your life so that you can have both sight and insight into God and your situation.

"While I am finishing up, I know some of you out there in the congregation still want to know what is the deal with Jesus using spit to heal the blind man so he could see and what is it with the reference to seeing men like trees walking. And while are at it, why did Jesus make the man look up not once but twice before the blind man could see everyone clearly?

"The answer in short is this. There are people in this life who will treat you like spit. There are also people in this world who will try to treat you as though you are less than and don't have any value. On top of that there are some people who based upon what they did or tried to do to you, it was so disrespectful that their actions were as though they were spitting on you. They had a total disregard for you and your feelings. Matter fact, some of those same people, if you are like me, are not only outside the church doors, but they are sitting right here in Mount Caramel Baptist church staring at me in my face and sucking their teeth, but I don't care. I'm just going to keep on telling it like it is.

"God lets you know that He is so powerful that He can even use the spit of life to give you sight. That's right. I'm not saying that what certain people tried to do to you is right. What I'm saying is that God has a way of taking the spit that comes your way in life and using that for you to be better able to see yourself and the people around you. God can use everything to bless you, but that should never be confused with everything being good. Evil is evil. Good is Good. The Scripture actually speaks to the power of God and that all things work together for good for those who love the Lord and are the called according to His purpose.

"I can't go on without sharing something about me that many of you may not know. I'm going to give you access not only to me as Pastor David Josiah Goodwell, but a closer understanding of me as DJ. My nickname in the neighborhood growing up back in the day was DJ. If you're thinking people called me DJ because of the initials of my name or because of how smooth my turntable mixing skills were in getting people out on the dance floor at the local club, then you would be dead wrong. The reason people called me DJ was because of my deadly jump shot. I could shoot a basketball with deadly accuracy from any place on the court. It didn't matter if it was indoor courts with hardwood floors or outdoors on asphalt with no net and a chain link fence, when I pulled up for a three-pointer, all you would hear after the ball went swish through the net, was 'DJ. DJ. DJ.'

"With each basket I scored, high school records were broken, city and state championship banners were hung up, and the expectations of my future as a professional basketball player continued to grow. Unfortunately, I went from breaking scoring records to hanging out with convicted felons with records. With each newspaper article, magazine cover or television reports, my notoriety grew larger than life, and so did my ego, feeling of self-importance and poor decision-making.

"In celebration of my being selected during my freshman year in college as 1st team All-American, a party was thrown in my honor in the VIP section of a club called G-spot. All I could see in the midst of all the champagne bottles popping and scantily-clad women were images of power, wealth and fame, but before the morning broke, all hell broke out. Instead of champagne bottles popping, gunshots popped in every direction. Right before my eyes, power turned into problems, wealth into whores and fame into felons.

"During that night a barrage of high caliber bullets shattered my right knee and ankle as well as my dreams to officially announce my intentions to leave college early for the NBA. My recuperation was difficult and arduous. It took a lot of hard work, determination and focus, but I eventually made it back to the basketball team and even had a successful college career full of many memorable games before I graduated with a double major. But deep down I was mad at God.

"I had made certain choices in life that clearly were not consistent with what God would have wanted for me to do, but despite the fact a major factor in my frustration with life was because of my having been blinded by sin and temptation, I nonetheless

103

blamed God for my predicament. I even decided that I was going to try to make it on my own without God.

"One night during an annual business retreat for corporate executives, I stood on the balcony of a plush hotel suite by myself, overlooking scenic mountains and towering trees. Dressed in a tailor-made tuxedo, I reflected on all the numerous awards I had received during the evening banquet. I was professionally successful by all accounts, but what people could not see that night was the level of emptiness I felt emotionally, physically and spiritually. I knew that overwhelmingly what people saw was a mirage of a person. I also knew right then that I needed to repair my relationship with God and acknowledge my sinful past as well as repent for my misplaced anger towards God.

"With tears in my eyes, I prayed to God that I might see the true purpose that God had for my life. When I raised my head up from praying, what I saw first were men like trees walking. When I sought God for further prayer and looked up again, I not only understood what my purpose was in life, I saw more clearly everyone around me.

"What God revealed to me then and reminded me before I spoke with you today is that the blind man was not born blind but once could see, and that is why he was able to identify the trees by sight. The blind had lost his sight somewhere and somehow on his life's journey. And if we are honest with ourselves, some of us have lost our sight somewhere in our journey.

"God lets the blind man know and lets us know that if you lost your way and can't figure out how you're going to make it, or because of sin you can't see what God has in store for your life the way that you once could, God lets us know that your sight can be restored. I was once blind, but now I see.

"There is one last message. It may not come all at one time. The healing of the blind man in this story is the only example in the Bible of God healing a man in stages. In this microwave, Internet, text message world of instant access and gratification, there is a false perception that everything happens right away.

"The reality is that some levels of pain don't disappear or go away right away. It occurs in stages. The promise of God is not that the hurt, hardship or headaches of life won't come your way nor that they will disappear instantaneously because you have a relationship with Jesus Christ. The promise is that you will be healed.

"God also revealed to me as a man of God that what we as a church community are lacking is large numbers of men who like trees are willing to stand tall and erect with the power and strength that can come only from God. Men of God who are not only strong men but deeply rooted in His Holy Word. We need men like trees walking in our communities.

"Some of you are saying, 'Pastor, what should I do right now?' Well, I tell you what I'm doing and what God has told me to share with you. First, accept Jesus Christ as Lord and Savior. Second, make sure that your hand and your life are being led by God and not by others. Thirdly, remember that your blind state is only temporary. If you walk with God, then God will give you both insight and sight, and lastly, you got to keep your head up.

"You can't see what God is doing in your life if you got your head down. The rapper Tupac used to have a song called 'Keep Your Head Up.' Thousands of years before Tupac, a man of God called Moses was leading his people through a treacherous desert and was following a pillar of cloud by day and a pillar of fire by night. Moses in the midst of the burning heat and the blistering hot desert sand kept his head up. What I've learned is you can't follow where God is taking you unless you got your head up. So to all the people who want to know how they are going to make it and to all the people who wonder how I am going to make it, here is the answer. Keep your head up. Stand Strong. Be deeply rooted in God's Word. Keep your hand and your life in Jesus' hand, and you can handle whatever comes your way. Amen."

CHAPTER THIRTEEN

I done told you before. Don't have no ho calling this house. Do you hear me? You ain't going to be disrespecting me like that. The least you could do with your trifling self is make sure that whatever ho you messing around with don't call my house or even have my telephone number. 'Cause I'm not tolerating no hoes calling my house, scratching up my car, or showing up on my doorstep. Am I making myself clear?"

"Monica, I don't know what you're talking about. You tripping."

"To hell with I'm trippin'. I'm not stupid, so don't try to make it out like I'm paranoid, 'cause I'm not," snapped Monica while frantically pointing her finger in the face of the man she had recently renewed a relationship with.

"Listen here. I'm not putting up with this nonsense. I don't know who has been calling your house and hanging up. But what I do know is you got less than one second to get your finger out my face."

"I put up with a lot of your nonsense, Steven, including the fact that you got a wife, but I am not going to tolerate you cheating on me. Period. Do you understand me?"

"Are you saying Crystal is calling you on the phone and hanging up? 'Cause, I don't believe that for one moment," Steven

Calloway replied while pushing Monica's hand away.

"Did I say it was Crystal? Did you hear me say her name in this house? I work for the woman. If your wife thought you were having an affair with someone, then she would have told me about it. She tells me all the dirt that you do. I know it's not her 'cause I still got a job and we're scheduled to go to the spa this weekend."

"So if it's not my wife, then who are saying that's calling?"

"That's what I'm asking you, Steven. I'm a woman. I know when another woman is calling my house. I done picked up the phone too many times and said hello and nobody said anything back before hanging up for it to be some wrong number. Now tell me what the hell is going on."

"Come on, baby. Why you being so difficult? I told you. Ain't nothing going on. I don't have no reason to lie to you," said Steven as he attempted to wrap his arms around Monica's waist.

"Don't touch me. You make me sick."

"Why you acting like this? I told you before. You're my one and only. From the first moment I saw you, I knew that we were meant to be together. I'm not going to do anything to jeopardize what we have. I believe in you and me."

"Don't lie to me. I've had enough of your lies and broken promises."

"I'm not lying to you, baby. If anybody knows my business and my whereabouts, it's you. If I'm not stuck at the office, a production shoot or some event that you placed on Crystal's schedule that I have to go to with her, then you know where I'm at. I'm always trying to be with you."

"When are we going to back to the Caribbean?" pouted Monica while folding her arms across her chest.

"Come on now. You know we could have gotten caught. We have to be smarter than that," frowned Steven while staring at Monica in disbelief. "You can't take off sick days and then fly down to a video shoot that I'm having and risk us being seen together. The best move, if you're serious about us going somewhere and spending quality time without us running into problems, then what you need to do as Crystal's chief of staff is pick an exotic place for a video shoot for one of our artists and bring a guy along with you on the trip."

"I don't get down like that. What type of woman do you think I am?"

"I'm not talking about you having sex with him, Monica. Y'all don't even have to sleep in the same room. You just need to be traveling together as though you're interested."

"I don't know about all that."

"Sweetheart, trust me. It'll work. All you have to do is just invite that uppity cornball Courtland with you on the trip and we'll be straight. You don't even have to give him none. Just make him think that he may get it. That plastic wannabe will front like he had sex with you to everyone on the trip just to save face and pretend that he's the man."

"And what about you? Are you going to be have sex with Crystal while we're on our trip? 'Cause I don't appreciate that."

"Of course not, baby, only if I have to. I don't like being with her that way. I just don't want for us to create unnecessary suspicion in her mind. Do you know what I'm saying?" said Steven while caressing Monica's hand. "After all the special time that we spent together, I know you have to know when I'm with her it is only about sex. No emotions, just sex. I don't love her. I love you and you only."

"Steven, I'm not sure that I can go along with that arrangement."

"What do you mean you're not sure? You know what my situation is. If I was to divorce her right now she would get not only half of all my money but half of the company, the company that you and I have worked so hard to build. I can't let that happen, sweetie, and by the way, I understood it when you slept with Courtland, even if I didn't agree with it."

"You have a lot of nerve. The only reason I slept with Courtland was in order to get you the information you wanted."

"Hold it one minute. Let's set the record straight, Monica. I never ever asked you to sleep with Courtland. I asked you to let that pompous Courtland character take you out on a date a couple of times so you could access his political connections at the mayor's office."

"Don't play dumb, Steven. You know damn well it was going to take more than me going out to a dinner, a play or getting drinks for me to find out what the deal is behind the money laundering charges being pursued by the mayor's office against Calloway Enterprises."

"I didn't say for you not to flirt, show off your legs or even wear a low-cut blouse and let him get a little peek, but I never said for you to have sex with him."

"You're right, Steven. You never said it, but don't pretend that you didn't know all along it might come down to that when you first asked me. You know and I know for a fact that status-conscious Courtland as a special assistant to the mayor was not going to be snooping around government files, Xeroxing classified documents and hacking computers unless he was certain I was going to give him some and it was going to be worth the wait."

"Well, I can vouch that it is worth the wait, but that doesn't mean you had any right giving it to him," responded a flustered Steven while shaking his head profusely in disappointment. "You should have just kept teasing him and then eventually told him when he invited you to his place after some foreplay that you were on your period."

"Yeah right, like that would have mattered to him."

"Well it matters to me," shouted Steven in disgust.

"Let me tell you something, Steven. You are not going to be leaving from your wife's bed on many a nights, then come over to my house to have sex with me and all of sudden want to sound prudish about what you find inappropriate and what you don't. I did what needed to be done for you and Calloway Enterprises, and just like you tell me, baby, it's just sex, not love."

"Point taken, Monica, point well taken. I can't argue with that. So why don't we switch subjects. What additional information have you been able to get out of Courtland?"

"Not so fast, Steven. You're not going to accuse me of being some two-bit ho and think I'm going to let that slide."

"Baby, I didn't say anything like that. I'm just sensitive about anybody, let alone that fake gigolo Courtland, touching the woman I love. Matter fact, you should actually have a bigger problem with me if I don't get upset about someone being with you intimately," reasoned Steven as he gave Monica a sappy eye look and extended his muscular arms to give her a big, gigantic hug.

"Now that's what I'm talking about, baby. If you keep squeezing me like that, I will tell you whatever you want to know."

"Monica, you so crazy," teased Steve before placing a long, sensuous tongue kiss on Monica that not only lifted her off her feet but placed her in such a state of ecstasy that anything Steven wanted to know or get was totally his.

"Steven, listen, baby, I need to tell you something important before we go any further and I forget," said Monica trying to regain some level of composure and decorum. "Your son, Shelton, has been leaking information to the FBI and is a key source of a secret indictment that will charge Calloway Enterprises and the owners of the G-spot Strip Club as co-conspirators in a money laundering scheme to use drug profits to purchase real estate in that newly regentrified community on the south side of town."

CHAPTER FOURTEEN

C rystal, don't you agree that the steel iron gates and newly constructed eight-foot brick wall encompassing our gated community serve as boric acid for the undesirable, non-ambitious, handout-loving, constant-excuse-providing, shiftless Black people," joked a pretentious real estate mogul who owned a substantial stake in the city's urban renewal plans.

Sitting next to me contouring her lips into a smirk before taking a sip of expensive Chardonnay was my recently-acquired powerhouse lawyer and new socialite, De'Borah Harriston, Esq. Before I could even counter the real estate tycoon's tasteless comment, De'Borah sarcastically asked him if as a slum lord didn't he need to be out somewhere evicting somebody in order to pay for another one his gaudy six button suits. The look of embarrassment on the tacky-dressed elitist wannabe was so entertaining I couldn't help but burst into a much-needed hearty laugh as he quickly shuffled away from our secluded table in the velvet roped off section of the trendy upscale restaurant.

It had been a while since I had been able to smile let alone laugh. The immense stress and toil of having to keep the dark secret that I killed Evelyn James was compounded by the reality that Mount Caramel Baptist Church Board of Trustees Chairman Paul Howard and his cronies were now blackmailing me and

113

threatening to kill my son and mother if I didn't cooperate.

My conscience as a loving mother who only wanted the best for her child without sacrificing my own life was heavily dependent on my acquiring for my son a top-notch legal team chaired by a take-no-prisoners chief counsel. I desperately needed someone who could handle the media frenzy and all the dirty tactics that the District Attorney was using to falsely convict my Shelton of murder in the court of public opinion.

Attorney Harriston not only came highly-recommended by some of the nation's most powerful law firms for her intellect and negotiating skills, but also was renowned in the business world for her unwavering commitment to winning tough cases. In the short time that we spent together getting acquainted, I was gaining a great level of respect not only for her legal acumen, but also her great listening skills. It didn't hurt that we looked like sisters and she had an impeccable taste in designer clothes.

With tears swelling in my eyes and feeling emotionally-vulnerable, I said, "De'Borah, you don't have any idea how thankful I am for your willingness to help me during this terrible ordeal. Having someone of your caliber defending my son makes a big difference, and I just want to say thank you."

"Crystal, don't cry. Do you hear me? Don't cry. I told you when we first met that I believed you when you said your son is innocent, and I need for you to believe me when I say I will not allow for an innocent child to go to prison for a murder that he did not commitment."

"You have no idea the level of stress and problems that I've been facing. This has been an enormously difficult time for me. I really appreciate all that you're doing. It feels good to have someone in my corner."

Before the first tear that had already fallen down the right side of my cheek could have company, De'Borah said, "Crystal, I am dead serious. Don't cry, even if you want to. We are out in public. You of all people should know that paparazzi are lurking everywhere. I need you to keep it together. Matter fact, take my sunglasses and act as though you are trying them on."

De'Borah's counsel could not have been more fortuitous. Staring directly at me from across the restaurant was none other than Vanessa Ford-Goodwell and her entourage of kiss-ups whose only claim to fame was that they were the sidekicks of a pastor's wife who was running for the state senate seat.

Clearly her calling me a witch behind my back on numerous occasions was obviously untrue due to the fact that she and her groupies didn't magically disappear or vaporize despite me blinking my eyes several times, nor were they suddenly swallowed up by a big gigantic pit and crushed by falling rocks. Instead, they sauntered their pompous way over to my table.

"Good afternoon, Sista Crystal. It is so good to see you," fawned Vanessa while looking me up and down to see if I was wearing anything fashionable that she did not already possess or want.

I responded by looking at her in a way that said that being married to a pastor may make you a first lady but it doesn't make you a lady—let alone a classy one. I then said, "How are you, Sista Ford, I mean, Sista Vanessa."

With no hint of the inherent disdain between us, she replied, "I'm not just doing good, I'm doing well. Matter fact, life is so great and God is so good that my last name is Goodwell."

I had expected a variety of smart aleck replies, but that one definitely caught me off guard. All I could do was foster a sheepish grin and remind myself that most marriages last shorter than a car note, and the word around town was her marriage to DJ had less staying power than the latest hip-hop artist.

"Crystal, I see you're having one of the chef's specially prepared dishes. The lemon pepper grilled salmon with cashews and raspberry vinaigrette is one of my all-time favorites. Clearly all the events that have been occurring in your life haven't dampened your appetite for a good meal."

"No, it hasn't. By the way, I see you have put on a couple of pounds. You aren't pregnant by any chance, are you?"

The way Vanessa gritted at me as I took my knife to cut another bite of the luscious salmon, you could envision her fantasying how wonderful it would be to take a butcher's knife, stab me in the heart and then twist it.

Instead, she ignored my comment and said to my new best friend, De'Borah, "We haven't had the pleasure of being introduced. My name is Vanessa Ford-Goodwell, and I am running for the newly-created state senate seat. I would be honored if you and Crystal would attend a reception that is being held for me this evening by the Women's Business Council." She then handed both of us a gold foil invitation envelope that was supposed to have all of the details.

Despite the wall of superficial irrelevance that her entourage made standing behind her, I could still make out a hostess waving in the background attempting to acquire their attention in order to notify them that a table was finally ready.

Just as quick as she gave me the invitation, I immediately flung it on the table as a sign of my disinterest. As the invitation settled between the half-empty water goblet and the Egyptian linen decorative napkin, I proudly informed her that the First Central Church Women's Day Committee was meeting this evening in preparation for the "Ladies in White" church program and tea. Therefore, I would be unable to attend her shindig. I then replied, "I hope you understand."

Vanessa begrudgingly took back the invitation but not without saying in a smug manner, "No problem, Crystal. I understand you don't want to miss out on finally having an opportunity to wear white in church."

Enough is enough, was the first thing that came to my mind. It was no secret that when I was pregnant with Shelton and showing, Steven and I got married. Therefore, despite my having always envisioned walking down the middle of the church aisle in front of hundreds of family and friends in a beautiful custom-made satin lace white wedding dress with a long train, I decided it was more appropriate to wear a tastefully embroidered ivory dress during a small ceremony attended by a select number of close friends.

Vanessa knew she was way out of line. It was totally inappropriate and ironic that a no-good chick like Vanessa who couldn't find Genesis nor Revelation in the Bible would be trying to play all sanctimonious. I desperately wanted to tell her that you think you know me but you really don't know me. On top of that, I wanted to let Vanessa know in no uncertain terms, with her arrogant, self-righteous, know-it-all persona, that just because you sleep with a pastor, sit next to the pulpit and wear fancy pearls, that don't mean you gonna make it through the pearly gates.

Instead, with a smile I murmured under my breath, "You fake evangelist wannabe." Apparently my murmur wasn't as soft as I thought because a scowl suddenly started appearing on several of Vanessa's assistants.

"What did you say?" Vanessa asked as though she was daring me to repeat it.

Not one to back down from a verbal confrontation, I momentarily leaned back into the swanky designer restaurant chair, sighed for a second before clearing my throat and my consciousness of all the mean-spirited things I was preparing to unleash on a woman who deserved it and more. In the midst of my making direct eye contact with Vanessa and everyone in her entourage, I felt De'Borah pinch my right upper thigh under the table.

With my focus momentarily shifted towards the sudden throbbing pain emanating from the welt on my leg, Attorney Harriston graciously said to Vanessa, "I would be honored to attend. Thank you so much for the invitation."

"You look familiar. Have we met before?" replied Vanessa to De'Borah's acceptance to attend the evening fundraiser.

"No. Not exactly. I did sing at your church recently during the pastoral anniversary. I was a guest of Reverend Reginald Walker. I must say you have a wonderful church," complimented Attorney Harriston with a broad smile.

"I knew you looked familiar," said Vanessa in an approving way. "What an awesome voice you have. It is my sincere hope that you will join us again for church."

"I appreciate your invitation and will definitely keep it in mind," responded De'Borah.

"Well. I look forward to seeing you tonight. If we don't get a chance to converse this evening, make sure that when you visit Mount Caramel, you notify the senior usher that you are my guest so that you will be brought down to the front rows. I know the congregation would love to be blessed by your singing once again," cajoled Vanessa before briskly walking away to her table with the entourage in tow.

Without even a goodbye or a wave, Vanessa was gone. I hadn't even gotten the chance to ask her whether or not Mount Caramel was a church or a club with all the talk about check with the senior usher, or should I say bouncer, when you come to the church. For the life of me, I still can't figure what DJ sees in her and why, of all people, he married her.

"What's wrong?" inquired De'Borah.

I didn't know that my body or facial expressions had given away that I was nervous until I noticed my right leg shaking profusely under the table. The sight of the television cameramen and reporters jostling for curb space outside the restaurant would have been enough to have me on edge, but the sudden appearance of police officers blocking the entrance and exit doors was making me jittery.

As I quickly tried to concoct a response to De'Borah's question, my cell phone rang, flashing a familiar number on my caller ID. I smiled apologetically to De'Borah because of the interruption, yet gratefully took the call.

"Attorney Calloway." I said as I covertly pressed the volume button to lower the sound so that De'Borah would not be able to make out anything that the caller said.

"Attorney Calloway, this Robert Vilcano of Vilcano Investigative and Protection Services."

"Yes. How are you?"

"You had said that as soon as I had any breaking news to let you know."

"Yes. Those were my instructions," I replied while pasting a pleasant smile on my face. No matter what he said, I told myself, don't let your façade crack.

"With regard to the text messages stating that your husband was going to divorce you, as you will recall, we had discovered that at least one of those messages could not have been sent by Evelyn James because of her traveling by airplane at the time."

"I do recall that."

"We now have irrefutable evidence that each of those text messages from Evelyn James was a fake. The messages you received were in fact sent to you from a disposable phone and made to look like they came from Mrs. James's phone using an encryption program."

"Very interesting," I blandly commented as my eyes nervously tracked the policemen's movements in and around the restaurant.

"Not only that, I think I may be able to uncover whose credit card was used to purchase that cell phone, and we should be able to corroborate that information using security video footage from the store."

"When would you anticipate having that information?"

"It may take a few days. But I also have additional great news to share. I have learned from contacts in law enforcement that there is evidence validating your son Shelton's statement that he was not present at the time of Mrs. James's murder. And it looks like they may possibly have either a new suspect or an accomplice, the source wasn't clear. In either case, they have at least one person underneath heavy surveillance and a warrant for their arrest is pending a judge's signature. My source could not give me the name on the warrant but did indicate that it would be a shocker."

"Very good. Thank for you the information, and please call me as soon as you have anything additional to share." Closing my phone, I gave De'Borah a wide, confident smile while internally I secretly begged, "Please, God, don't let them take me outta here like a common thief."

CHAPTER FIFTEEN

Love without you is like a heart without a beat, a song without sound, breath without life. It has no meaning or value unless you are a part of it. For life has taught me that for many people, love is a mere word, a feeling, an expression of gratitude or term of endearment, but for you and I, love is an action, a way of life. And every day I wake up and go to sleep committed to that action, to that life, to you and only to you," whispered a sincere Jordan Clark to his beloved wife Theresa Hall.

"Wow...I don't know what to say. Sometimes you just take my breath away," cooed Theresa while listening to Jordan passionately express his unwavering devotion to their marriage.

"Listen, sweetheart, I can't be on the phone long, but in light of what happened the last time I was out of town, I wanted to share with you how important our relationship is to me and that I won't allow for anyone or anything to come between us."

"Jordan, I have to be honest with you. I'm still a little uncomfortable with what happened when you returned home and how you responded to me."

"I respect that, and while we are being candid, I didn't feel the way you came at me, but when I stepped back from the situation and imagined how I would have felt if the situation was reversed, then I became less defensive and more understanding."

"Sweetheart, I love you, but you have to promise me that you will be more careful. Even as a Christian woman there is only so much I feel I can bear, and I don't want to be made a fool of."

"Nobody does."

"You're not understanding me, baby. I really need for you to listen to me," prayerfully requested a slightly exacerbated Theresa. "So many of my girlfriends are in unhealthy, self-destructive relationships. I am always getting flak about the fact that all men are dogs, including you."

"Who said that?" responded Jordan in an angry tone.

"That's not what's important. What is important is that I'm always taking up for you and telling them that it is possible to have a relationship that has mutual respect."

"Theresa, which one of your bitter girlfriends said something about me?"

"Baby, you're not hearing me. I'm trying to tell you something real important, and I really need for you to stay focused on what I am saying. 'Cause it's not about them, it's about us," said Theresa while starting to sob louder and louder.

"What's going on? What did I say? What did I do?" pressed Jordan as he flipped between concern and frustration.

"Sweetie, I don't like to bring this up because it's uncomfortable for me and a reminder of my past," Theresa began as she fought through the tears. "You know that when I was in college, for a short time, and I do mean a very short time, I worked in a gentleman's club."

"Why are you bringing this up? I told you before. That was before we knew each other. I don't like talking about it," fumed Jordan.

"Neither do I, but if you want to know why I was so upset, it was the fact that when you came home with that woman's lingerie in your suitcase, it made me think about all the unfaithful men that were married or in relationships that would be in the club every night."

"What does that have to do with me?"

"Nothing, Jordan, but it has a lot to do with me. While I know that God has forgiven me and I have given my life to Christ, I felt that all the dirt and poor decisions that I had made with other people's men had finally come back to me and taken the one man in my entire life that I trust. You, baby."

Theresa's vulnerability made Jordan soften. "Theresa, I need for you to pay close attention to me. I'm not perfect and you're not perfect, but we serve a perfect God. God has a history of using and reclaiming people who other people would have given up on or never given a chance." Sensing that his words were providing comfort to his wife, Jordan continued. "Abraham was a liar; Jacob was a trickster; Noah was a drunk; Moses was a murder; David was an adulterer; Samson was a ladies man; Matthew was an extortionist. Saul, before he became Paul, persecuted Christians, but God used Paul when he was willing to accept Jesus Christ as Lord and Savior to not only spread the Word of God, but to write the majority of the books in the New Testament. What I am saying, baby, is this: God has a way of redeeming people, including you and me, if we give our life to God. And I'm thankful that both you and I have done exactly that."

"Jordan, you don't know how much you mean to me," responded Theresa while trying to regain her composure.

"I love you, too, baby, but I got to go."

"Why?" Theresa whined. She didn't want their intimate moment to end.

"The meeting is getting ready to begin, and I need to be in there."

"Who are you meeting with again?"

"I can't say, baby."

"What do you mean you can't say?"

"Exactly as I said. I can't say and that is all I'm gonna say about it," said Jordan with a stronger tone than he felt deep down, but he needed to get the point across to Theresa that the topic was not up for discussion.

"Don't you trust me? We're married," questioned Theresa in an attempt to play on his feelings.

"It's not about that."

"Then what is it about? I don't understand you," huffed a flustered Theresa. "You want me to trust you, but you won't trust me. I don't know why you can't see the contradictions."

"I'm not denying that there's a contradiction, but this isn't about us. It is about work, and it's better for the both of us that we keep those two worlds separate."

"You sound just like my brothers. Y'all are alike. It doesn't matter if you're slinging dope in the shadows or pushing political candidate agendas in the dark. It's all shady. If you can't do it in the light, then you ain't living right."

"I'm not agreeing or disagreeing. I'm just saying that this isn't the time. By the way, have you heard from your brother, Prince Murda?"

"Don't call him that. His name is Prince. Prince Hall. Not Prince Murda, not Murda P or any other name or title that associates him with wrongdoing," retorted an agitiated Theresa.

"I wasn't trying to be offensive. I was just trying to genuinely express a level of concern for him," snapped Jordan. "I think he's a cool dude who just needs some additional direction."

"What are you trying to say about me and my family?" Theresa asked defensively.

"Slow your roll, baby. It is not even like that. I just see a lot in the brother," responded Jordan, attempting to deflate what was meant as a compliment versus a slur.

"That's because both of y'all are gangsters. Just in two different fields."

"I'm not even going to dignify that with a response. I'm just going take it as an inappropriate joke and keep it moving."

"Naw. Don't let it pass," jokingly shot back Theresa. "Whether it is drug dealing, the music business or politics, all of you are dealing in the underworld with shady people."

"I don't receive that. I just play the game with the rules that have been made."

"And what is the difference between what you're saying and what my brother Omar, my brother Kevin, Prince or any other brother out there hustling says?"

"There is a big difference between what they do and what I do, and it seems ludicrous to me that you would even compare us."

"You getting a little sensitive there," kidded Theresa.

"I'm not sensitive. I just don't appreciate what you said," replied Jordan while checking his watch to time his arrival at the meeting. "So have you heard from Prince or not?"

"No, I haven't. I left him several messages, and he hasn't responded. I'm just keeping him up in my prayer. When dealing with him, who knows what's going on."

"Okay, I gotta go."

"Hold on, Jordan, before you leave. I don't pretend to know as much about politics as you nor do I claim to be as interested as you would like for me to be, but I do know this. Ever since you got more heavily involved with this upcoming presidential election, you started going to church less often."

"It is not that simple."

"Then tell me this. Are we going to the First Central Church revival this week?"

"I'm not sure, baby. I have a lot on my plate."

"See what I mean. The revival is five days," pushed an irritable Theresa while sighing deeply. "You surely should be able to make it at least one day."

"Let me get back to you on that," whispered Jordan as he approached the conference room door.

"Well. I want for us to go to First Central Church together. I am tired of people asking me where my husband is."

"It is none of their business where I'm at."

"Husbands and wives should be in church together. You of all people know that," huffed Theresa before saying, "I am going to pray for you and even ask Bishop Jackson to pray for you, the same way I've been having him pray for Prince."

"Look, Theresa, I'm not going to argue with you. I love you and I love God. We are just in two different places right now."

"Jordan, don't let whatever you're into come between you and church. Do you hear me? Bishop Jackson is a good pastor and a good man who is doing a lot for the community. Do you see how big the church has gotten? They are building a new sanctuary to accommodate all the people who are joining First Central. That is proof alone that Bishop Jackson is doing God's work. "

"Sweetie, you don't get it, but I love you, and I mean that," stressed Jordan before abruptly hanging up the phone. The meeting time had arrived, and there were a lot of issues that Jordan needed to sort out.

Jordan understood that because of his political prowess and ingenuity he had been recruited to mastermind a public relations campaign to bring down the Black male Democratic presidential candidate. The political kingmakers knew that destroying the Black candidate was pivotal to the white female Democratic presidential candidate's ability to win the party nomination. Even though she wasn't liked by many of the key players in her own party, a group of Democratic political kingmakers strategized that she was the best chance they had of beating a white male Republican candidate to regain the presidency.

It was imperative that the operation not be traceable to the white Democrats or key members of the Democratic party who hired him. Prominent white Democrats could not be seen attacking a Black man running for the presidency of the United States. This was especially the case given the Black candidate's celebrity glow and magnetism. If Black women suspected that white Democrats were behind the attacks, then their coveted vote could never be manipulated to support the white female candidate.

To complicate the Democrats' plans, Republicans were secretly funneling large sums of money into the Black male candidate's coffer. Their strategy was to strengthen the Black candidate's challenge to the white female frontrunner during the primaries to undermine her appeal to Black voters. If the Democrats could be divided now, then the Republicans could conquer them in November.

Jordan knew that one of the most important keys to his success rested on which candidate would receive the influential endorsement of a group of prominent Black pastors known as the Preachers' Syndicate. The Preachers' Syndicate was a secret society of corrupt pastors whose support was so powerful it could alter the election landscape across the country during any key election.

As Jordan entered the dimly lit conference room, a burly bodyguard asked him to place all of his phones and any other form of electronic device into a basket. He was then told to assume the position as the muscle-bound sentinel frisked him and checked his clothes for any recording or listening devices. He directed Jordan to take a seat at the nearest armchair.

Suddenly, the room went dark. Jordan began to jump up. "Stay still," the security guard commanded. Reluctantly, Jordan acquiesced recognizing the importance of his mission.

The door on the far side of the room cracked open. A tall man with broad shoulders approached Jordan. Due to the darkness, Jordan could not make out who it was, although he thought he recognized the man's confident, authoritative gait. The sentinel respectfully pulled out the black leather chair for the man to sit down at the head of the table. The lights came on. Blinking, Jordan's initial thought was confirmed. A gentleman in an expensive, tailor-made suit with a matching monogrammed shirt and tie folded his arms on the table and said, "It's been brought to my attention that we may have some mutual interests and friends."

Jordan would have wanted to be surprised, but unfortunately he wasn't. The man across the table from him was none other than his wife's favorite pastor, Bishop Jackson.

CHAPTER SIXTEEN

If you don't remember anything else that I tell you today, this much is undeniable," I began while my nephew Shelton attempted to figure out a way to stop me from shooting another jump shot straight through the net. "In order for you to make it out of situations where you are trapped and being held in bondage to a place where you are free to live out God's promises for your life, then there is a lesson from Moses's leadership in the book of Exodus you need to take to heart."

With a lightning first step, I made a move to my favorite spot on the basketball court. Shelton, trailing me, was clearly unfazed, however I could still hear him begrudgingly murmur, "Good move."

I slowed down with a stutter step so Shelton could be dead center in front of me. "You have to understand that between slavery in Egypt and freedom in the promise land was a desert. How you deal and persevere through your life's deserts knowing that God will be faithful and provide for you will determine whether you make it to your promise land or not."

I then accentuated my point with a fade-away, turn around jumper from the top of the key that went straight through the net without touching the rim. "Remember this. Godly delay does not mean God's denial."

"That was a lucky shot," shouted Shelton.

"You better recognize and play some better D," I shot back while waving for him to pass me the leather ball.

"Uncle DJ, you know that was luck. Stop playing like you got it like that."

"Ain't nothing changed. I've been using that move since before you were even born. That is what you call old school."

"You just old. I'm in school," laughed Shelton as he positioned himself in front of me in a defensive posture by waving his lanky arms and bending his knees.

In a braggadocios way, I said, "With God, it is never too late, but as for this basketball game, I'm about to put you out of your misery."

"You wish," grimaced Shelton as he purposefully pushed me in my back twice in order to throw me off my balance while I dribbled the ball near the three-point line.

"I like that. I like that," I repeated. "You think that just because you give me an elbow here and there or push me that I'm going to get distracted. Naw, baby. I'm focused on the end result. Those petty fouls you're doing are just delaying the inevitable."

"We'll see," declared Shelton as he made a daring lunge to swipe the ball away from me.

"See ya." Replicating an earlier move, I quickly spun away from him and started dribbling as fast as I could to my favorite spot on the basketball court. Shelton in hot pursuit was drenched in sweat from our hours of playing Horse and one-on-one. In a last second adjustment, I decided that instead of taking one of my infamous deadly jumpers from deep in the corner, I would make a sudden dash straight to the hoop for a dunk.

Surprised by my bold move, Shelton screamed out, "Oh no, you won't," as he accelerated behind me into warp speed. The adrenalin was tremendous. Both of us were racing at top speed for a showdown in the air. Early in the game, Shelton had done both a tomahawk dunk and reverse double pump dunk after crossing me up with a trick dribble. This was going to be my chance to pay him back.

When we first began, Shelton was showboating in every way imaginable. Every basketball move he made was an attempt to end up on ESPN's Play of the Day. Unfortunately, for all the shaking and baking and fancy moves that Shelton made before he shot the ball, several of his dunks at the end of the mind-numbing play did not go in the basket as intended.

Wham.

That was all you heard. The sound of the rim rattling and my swinging on it with my legs spread open was a surprise not only to Shelton but also to me. It had been a while since I had jumped that high in the air. All Shelton could do was start shaking his head from side to side in both admiration and shock at what would have been considered a nice slam even by his standards. He then said, "Let's play again. Best of three."

Exhausted and desperately needing water, I immediately waved Shelton off and said, "No more for me. What are you trying to do, kill me?"

Shelton's joyous facial expression sunk into a blank, vacant stare devoid of happiness. With a careless, playful remark, I had interrupted the loving time we had been sharing by reminding him of the reality that he was standing accused of Evelyn James's heinous murder.

Still in shock, but recovering from my thoughtless comment, Shelton nodded his head to let me know that we were cool.

"I didn't mean that," was all that I could think to say.

"I know you didn't," responded Shelton after dunking the ball with such authority you thought he was trying to tear down the rim.

"Shelton, let's take a break for a few minutes. I need to catch my breath."

"Cool," he said as he followed me over to the cooler packed with ice, water, sodas and energy drinks.

"How you holding up?"

"I'm doing what I got to do," he responded with a hardened tone, and then softened and said, "I'm keeping my head up, regardless of what's printed or on television. I know I didn't kill Evelyn. I actually loved her." He then leaned against the wall and stared at the ground.

"I can respect that."

"How about you, Uncle DJ?" questioned Shelton, looking me in the eye. "Your name's been up in the newspapers, too."

"True that." I nodded. "That is one of the reasons that I wanted for us to get together." I then sat down on the bleachers and leaned as far back as I could, making myself comfortable. "Shelton, I know that you see and read things in the news just like I do. In particular, I know that you've had to see the newspaper photos and articles where they talk about you being my son."

As soon as I began speaking, Shelton put his head into his hands. I could tell that the conversation was emotionally stressful for him.

"Look, nephew. I'm not trying to make what has been a difficult time harder." I sat up and turned towards him, resting my elbows on my knees. "I just felt a responsibility to our friendship to tell you man to man that I'm not your father, but if I was, I would be proud to have you as my son."

Despite the heaviness of the subject and my forthrightness, Shelton never once lifted up his head or said a single word to me. Deep down it pained me that even with all the love I had had for his mother years ago, we didn't work out. Crystal had been the love of my life in college, until she became pregnant by another man.

That, of course, was bad enough. But to make matters worse, Crystal had slept with my brother, married him, and for the longest had me believing that Shelton was Steven's child. Maybe I should have told my brother the truth about Shelton not being his son, but I never could forgive him for having sex with the woman I once loved. Both of them deserved the misery of each other.

Shelton interrupted my relationship flashbacks by saying jokingly, "Uncle DJ, you know my favorite newspaper photo is the one where they have you, me, and your brother side-by-side and then ask the readers to answer a poll saying which one of you I look more alike."

His comment stunned me, and I couldn't quite make out why he was laughing. I grinned anyway and said, "I know you don't get along with your father, but calling him 'your brother' and not 'my father' is taking it all a bit too far. Don't you think?"

"Uncle DJ, I'm not trying to be disrespectful, but there is a lot of baggage between the man and me that you don't know about it."

"What is causing for you to disrespect him like that?" I stared hard at Shelton trying to read his face.

"You don't really want to know that." He shook his head and looked out across the court.

"Yes. I do. Never, in all the time that you have known me, have I ever ducked anything nor taught you to duck anything. I always tell you to go hard."

"I don't know about this one." He glanced over at me to see if I was for real.

"Are you trying to tell me that your father is connected with Evelyn's murder?" I ventured.

"No. I'm not saying that."

"You haven't been saying a lot about how you're dealing with things."

"For the most part, Uncle DJ, I go to sleep every night hoping and believing that when I wake up the next day, Evelyn will be alive and this will all be a bad dream."

Silently nodding, I paused to allow his words to sink in. "So, what is it that you think I can't deal with?"

"Well, for one, the man my mother is married to is cheating on her."

I was torn between feeling on the one hand sorry for my nephew who, with all the troubles on his plate, had found out that Steven was having an affair, and on the other hand feeling happy that Crystal was experiencing some of the same pain she had given to me. Part of me wanted to laugh. Instead, I just listened.

"But Uncle DJ, that isn't even the worst of it."

"Shelton, do you think your mother knows?"

"I don't know, Unc. My mom has been so stressed out as of late with concern about me, I didn't want to add to her heartache by telling her something as painful as that." Shelton then paused and flipped the basketball in the air before saying, "Every time I talk to my mother, she's giving me updates on how great this new attorney is and trying to comfort me. I don't want to further upset her with bad news while she's all worried about me and trying to do everything she can to clear me of Evelyn's murder."

"I'm not defending my brother, but how do you know that he's having an affair?"

Shelton stopped spinning the basketball on his finger, placed it on the ground near him and said, "One night, I went to this hip underground lounge spot where a lot of drug dealers go to chill."

Angry and concerned, but at the same time appreciative of my nephew's honesty, I quickly respond, "What the hell were you doing there?"

"My man, Prince Murda, told me he knew the people that run it, and it would be safe."

"Shelton, I'm a little confused. I thought you and Prince Murda were enemies."

"Naw, Unc. Prince Murda and I are actually cool. We've had our ups and downs, but we've known of each other for years through playing basketball. The majority of what happens between us on mixtapes and radio interviews is primarily to sell records. Sometimes it may get out of control and people around us may escalate the situation, but Prince Murda and I usually arrange for a secret meeting to determine what's the real beef and what's made up hype."

"No matter," I replied, wanting to refocus the conversation. "It makes no sense that you were there. What were you thinking?"

"To be real with you, Uncle DJ, that's what I wanted to ask your brother. 'Cause as much as my moms has given to support him and the family business, I wanted to say to him, 'What are you doing with that chick on her knees in the corner booth? It doesn't make sense for you to be here. What are you thinking?' "

I shook me head at Steven's stupidity. "Your mother should have never gotten you involved in the music industry."

"Uncle DJ, I know you mean well, but it wasn't my mother's decision. It was mine."

"Even so, your mother knew better. She should have protected you."

"I know you don't really like my moms because of the history you have, but there is a lot you don't know."

"I can say same thing to you, youngin'. There is a lot you don't know about. Matter fact, I was disappointed when you didn't show up for the ribbon cutting ceremony for the community center named after your grandfather. It was the Reverend Cecil Goodwell who, despite all the issues that I've had with my brother and your mother, told me not to take out my frustrations against you."

"I didn't know that."

"There was no reason for you to know. All you needed to know growing up was that your Uncle DJ loved you and I would support you to whatever extent that you needed. When you were young and took an interest in basketball, that provided an additional hook to unite you and me together."

"There is still stuff, Unc, that either you're not telling me or you don't know. 'Cause the level of tension that exists between my moms and you is so thick." He looked me in the eye as if to determine whether I knew what he was talking about.

Not sure what Shelton was trying to get at, I took a deep breath and said, "Okay, how about this. Your moms, when she became pregnant, did not initially tell me that she was pregnant. Instead, when she was one or two months along she planned to sleep with me while I was home for the college break. If it wasn't for my moms, your grandmother, becoming sick, I would have gotten with your moms before I went back to college."

"I know about that."

"Do you now. Did you know that your father was always jealous of me growing up and that he knew your mother before I did but never dated her? One day he was telling me of this girl he had a serious crush on and wanted to be with. I didn't know it was your moms. Your moms and I met separately at a party. When I showed up with her at the house one day, your father went crazy. Claimed I had stolen his girl."

"Uncle DJ, I will take what you're saying to one more level. After that, your brother hated on you even more so that when my mother slept with him after you left for college, Steven was thrilled to be able to say that he was the one who was my father."

The realization of what Shelton had been trying to get at finally hit me, and the whole conversation was now starting to make sense. Shelton somehow knew that Steven wasn't his father. "How do you know all that?"

"That's not the point. The point is, either you don't know or you aren't telling me."

Once again confused, I replied, "I'm not sure what you want to know. Do you wanna hear that for the longest I hated on both my brother and your moms? Do you wanna know that I never told him that he wasn't your father? What do you want to hear from me?"

"I want for you to tell me who my father is," he demanded.

"Shelton, I don't know who your father is. I didn't even know that you knew that Steven wasn't your father."

"Don't lie to me, Uncle DJ." Shelton shook his head in disgust.

"I can't believe that you would come at me like that. I've always been up front with you."

"You never told me that your brother wasn't my father," he countered.

"I didn't believe that it was my place to say. To reveal something like that might seem like I was doing it out of hate or jealousy."

"I wanna believe you...." The pained look on Shelton's face cut me to the core.

"There is no wanting to believe me. Everything I'm telling you is the truth." I was now depending on my integrity and history of standing up for what is right no matter what the odds were to drive my point home for me.

"Uncle DJ, there is just something that I want to share with you, but I gotta believe that you are who you say you are." Shelton kept glancing at me, almost as if he thought his eyes were some sort of lie detector and he could read my integrity from my face.

I turned directly towards him and spoke with the utmost sincerity. "I am a strong man of God who tries to live his life in a way pleasing to God. I've always been real with you, Shelton. I love you because I see a lot of you in me. I can't see why you don't see or know that after all of these years."

"Okay, Uncle DJ, you made your point. I'm going to tell you

something that I'm not supposed to know."

"And what is that?"

"I know who my father is. It just hurts so bad that I didn't want to acknowledge it to be true. My mother doesn't even know that I know the story."

"So who is it?" I asked anxiously.

Shelton hesitated. "It's not that easy to say, so let me tell you this first. You have my mother wrong. She did what she felt that she had to do with the cards she was dealt. You think my moms cheated on you while you were in college, but she didn't. She was raped."

"She was raped? Where did you hear that?" Shocked, I mentally began trying to run through every interaction Crystal and I had had during that time. Was there anything to confirm what Shelton was saying? Had I really been so caught up in myself that I had completely missed the clues that would have pointed to her deep anguish and suffering?

"Never mind that. The fact is that she was raped and didn't know what to do and was scared. In retrospect, my moms would have told the police, but she was concerned that nobody would believe her, and she didn't want to be made out to be a villain."

"I would have believed her if she had told me," I stated emphatically. How could Crystal not have trusted me given the depth of the love we shared?

"You say that now, but you don't know that until you're placed in that situation. My moms was going to have an abortion, but she waited too long and it was just past three months, even though she wasn't showing it. That's why she slept with your brother."

"That doesn't make sense. If Crystal was raped, why would that make her decide to sleep with my brother?"

"Uncle DJ, have you ever wondered why we look so much alike even though you're not my father and your brother is not my father?

I scrutinized Shelton's face. What was he saying?

"Well, I'll tell you the reason why. Your father, my grandfather, raped my mother."

Incredulous, I jumped up. "No. Say it ain't so."

"See, Uncle DJ, that is exactly what my mother was afraid of. The Reverend was so popular, she didn't think anyone would believe her, so she first tried to get with you, and when that wasn't possible, she got with your brother. One way or another, she was determined that I would in some way look like the man who was my father."

It all seemed so unreal. How could my father, the Reverend Cecil Douglass Goodwell, have done this to me...to her? I wanted to scream. Instead I took the basketball and slammed it against the backboard. "Why are you telling me this? And why now?"

"I know it's a shock. I don't like facing it myself, but the way I see it, what's done is done. I'm telling you, not because of the past but the present. I'm letting you know because there are other things going on right now, and my moms said that if she had to do it over again, she would have told someone she trusted, who wouldn't be afraid to support her and would believe her."

"So what's your point?" I tried to regain my composure.

"A friend...," Shelton began tentatively, "Prince Murda knows something scandalous that I don't even know the full scoop on, and he doesn't know who he can trust. It's big, and it involves a lot of powerful people...."

"Who?" I was still reeling from the bomb Shelton had just dropped and struggling to erase from my mind the image of the evil my father had committed.

"I told him that he could trust my Uncle DJ, because he not only preaches about God but lives what he preaches."

I sighed deeply. If I thought I had wrestled before with resentment against Steven, this was on a whole different level. Rage welled up within me. If my father wasn't already dead.... "Shelton, who?" I demanded.

He scanned the gym for anyone possibly standing nearby, and then whispered, "It's concerning Bishop Jackson. Your life may be in danger."

CHAPTER SEVENTEEN

"Monica, I really need your honest opinion. What would you say if I told you I think Steven is having an affair?"

Crystal's tone of voice and body language sounded genuine and perhaps even vulnerable, but I still couldn't be certain if she suspected me of having an affair with her husband. Since I'd started sleeping with her Steven, I'd been secretly using our monthly get-togethers for spa treatments as a timeframe to gauge whether she suspected anything as well as to make sure she didn't.

No matter how careful I was, though, I knew there was always a chance of being exposed or caught. Had that day finally arrived?

"Girl, what are you talking about? You and Steven have the best relationship."

"I don't know. That's what I've thought and believed, too, over the years, minus the occasional music industry tramp that I and every other wife has had to deal with."

"Crystal, I had no idea that y'all were experiencing any problems."

"I don't have any proof, but my women's intuition keeps on talking to me. It's just a gut feeling that I have and haven't been able to shake."

"You haven't brought this up before," I probed. "How long have you felt this way?" Even with the stress-relieving aromatherapy candles infusing the room with sweetness, I could feel anxiety beginning to grip me. Stay cool, Monica, I tried to tell myself, while being wrapped from head to toe in hot towels.

"The feeling comes and goes. Sometimes I just dismiss it as being hypersensitive or overreacting to nothing. But other times I just can't ignore the fact that certain things just don't add up."

I immediately began doing calculations of my own. Did I overestimate Crystal's trust of Steven? Did my recent multiplied efforts to cover my own tracks backfire somehow? Were my recent demands for Steven to spend more time with me undermining my overall plan to steal her husband?

"Are you sure? Steven doesn't give me the impression that he's stepping out on you. At least that's what my women's intuition says. Especially with the way he looks at you."

"Hmm." She seemed to ponder my comment. "That's good to know, 'cause to be honest, I don't feel like he looks at me the way he once used to," Crystal said while examining her facial and body features in the ceiling mirrors. Inwardly, I smiled as I inspected my own youthful glow.

As we rose and prepared to follow the spa hostess to our respective massage rooms, I tried to reassure her. "You would know better than me, but I can say a lot of women would love to get the amount of attention you get. Didn't I see a couple dozen roses in your office?"

"My sweetie does keep my office looking and smelling beautiful, doesn't he?"

"See, girl. You don't have anything to worry about."

The sparkle in Crystal's eyes assured me that I had dodged a bullet. She probably thought my warm smile was meant to comfort her or in anticipation of the deep-tissue massage I had requested, but actually, I was congratulating myself. Earlier during the month, I had arranged for Crystal to receive a bi-monthly flower arrangement paid for by Steven's credit card. I never could have anticipated that the seeds planted by that simple gesture would bear so much beneficial and timely fruit.

Just as we were about to enter into our own massage suites, Crystal stopped abruptly and gently grabbed my arm. Her furrowed brow let me know that a new thought had entered her mind and was threatening to undermine the comfort the flowers brought her. "Monica, I know even as my girl this may be TMI, but Steven and our sex life isn't what it used to be. I even went out and bought a whole new drawer of lingerie."

My smile broadened. Steven had said he didn't feel anything when he had sex with his wife, that he only did it when he had to. He must really love me. "Have you spoken to him about it? It could just be the effects of stress or something health related," I added.

"You're probably right," she gladly conceded, but then suddenly turned back around and whispered, "Monica, you don't think that he caught something from some nasty two-bit ho and because of that he doesn't want to have sex with me. Do you?"

"No, girl. Don't think like that. You need to think positive and work through it."

As we entered our respective massage suits, a frown slightly crept across my face. Deep down I wanted to say to Crystal, "I know you ain't calling me no ho."

*　　*　　*

As the masseuse began kneading away at the knots of stress in my lower back, I reflected on Crystal's suspicions and my own choices and decisions to finally succumb to Steven's advances. I met Crystal on a return flight from a women's health and lifestyle enrichment conference sponsored by a consortium of fashion designers and advertising agencies. During a delay in the plane's departure, Crystal and I noticed our similar conference bags and struck up a conversation about how wonderful of a conference it was and that we both looked forward to attending next year.

Crystal, as it turned out, had been one of the small group leaders for a breakout session on relationships. I was moved to tears when she told me about a woman's journey from abuse victim to healing to being able to have a healthy, loving relationship. Until that point, I hadn't realized how deeply my own abusive relationship had damaged my soul and my self-esteem. I hate to cry among strangers, let alone in public, but that day the flow of tears refused to be quelled. Crystal gently put her hand on my shoulder and without missing a beat continued to share with me that my past was exactly that—my past, and it did not have to define my present nor control my future.

By the end of the flight, we spoke privately about my struggles and fears. When I told her that despite all of my education, I was in a dead-end job and had student loan and credit card debt higher than even the highest note a gay guy in church could sing, she then offered me a job as an executive-in-training at her law firm.

Even though Crystal eventually became my supervisor at the

firm as I moved up in rank and responsibilities, she and I still continued to grow closer over time. As her executive-in-training, we spent an enormous amount of time together, except, of course, when she was with her family. In some ways I idolized her. She seemed to have it all—a successful marriage, ambitious husband, money, prosperous business, talented son—you name it, the Calloways seemed to have it all, or so I thought.

One of the first indications I got that everything was not necessarily so great in her relationship with Steven was Crystal's refusal to attend the premiere of Steven's independent film, "The Revenge of the Booty Shakers," as well as its celebrity-packed after-party. In an act that was totally unsupportive of Steven, Crystal said she wasn't feeling well and needed rest and then later that same night was photographed by a leading newspaper socializing at the grand opening of an international art exhibit.

Despite Steven's professional success and the family business, it was clear that Crystal was embarrassed by him. On numerous occasions, even with her office door being tightly closed, I could overhear her making disparaging remarks to Steven about him not living up to her expectations. For the bulk of all the entertainment industry related events Steven wanted Crystal to attend, she declined to go, regardless of whether it could fit on her calendar. Over time, constantly telling Steven that Crystal was unavailable or had a last minute scheduling conflict made me actually start to feel sorry for him. Crystal didn't give him enough credit. He could never measure up to her notion of the ideal man.

Crystal's take all my calls rule and have people leave a message meant Steven and I often conversed on the phone. In all of our interactions he was always pleasant and friendly. When my former college roommate, Theresa Hall, did not return my phone calls concerning getting tickets from her brother, Prince Murda, for what was being billed as the greatest concert of the millennium, even though I had told her I'd promised relatives who were coming in from out of town that I could get tickets to this sold-out mega event, I took matters into my own hands.

I didn't want to let my nephews and nieces down nor look like a fool to several of my family members who doubted I could acquire the tickets since their muckety-muck connections hadn't resulted in a single lead. When Steven showed up at the firm in order to take Crystal out to lunch at one of the city's most popular restaurants as well as show off his brand new convertible, I decided to ask him if there was anyone he knew that I could purchase concert tickets from and it wouldn't send me into bankruptcy to buy them.

I told him up front that I would one hundred percent understand if he said no, because this was truly the most radio-hyped event of the century. Steven said he would look into it. To my heart-pounding surprise, two days later Steven not only had a messenger deliver to me tickets for great seats, but also the unthinkable: five backstage all-access passes.

Yes, yes, yes, is all I remember screaming in way all too reminiscent of a multiple orgasm that I had not had in years. My reputation as the greatest auntie alive would now not only remain true but would reach such unparalleled heights of appreciation that it would go unchallenged in my nephews' and nieces' lives forever.

I couldn't wait to thank Steven, no matter how much the concert tickets cost. When he phoned the next day and said the tickets were free and just a token of his gratitude for how nice I was on the phone when he called, I was smitten. Crystal had herself an awesome guy. Too bad she didn't see it that way.

The next morning, I walked into the firm and the entire office floor was in abuzz about the beautiful dozens upon dozens of roses that Crystal had adorning every table, bookcase and office ledge in her spacious office. "Damn," I thought to myself. "Crystal has it going on and just doesn't know how lucky she is." She doesn't have to deal with all the knuckleheads that I was running into or being introduced to. For a person who didn't even like to spend the extra time recycling my garbage, I had no problem recycling other people's relationship trash, is what I thought after my latest bad dating experience.

When Steven called that day to speak with Crystal, I immediately started gushing praise on him for having gotten me the concert tickets and how I would do anything to make it up to him. I then told him to hold one second and I would personally go get Crystal out of the staff meeting so that she could talk to him. Any man who would do all that he did for me and buy her that many gorgeous flowers is not being told that he will get a call back. That was my view, whether Crystal liked it or not.

Midway through my comments, Steven asked if I could attend a listening session for one of his artists as well as screen a movie trailer that was supposed to be going to theaters in the very near future. He said something about valuing my opinion in light of what I wear and listen to. He thought I had a magical finger on what today's market wanted to hear and see.

I told him thank you but that I wasn't sure how appropriate that would be in light of working for his wife and her views about some of the things he produced. I did end by saying I would definitely think about it and appreciated him seeing me in that light. I also told him that I thought the flowers he had gotten Crystal were beautiful and that everyone on the staff was lavishing praise about them. To my surprise, he said the flowers had been meant for me, not Crystal.

If anyone had gotten a glimpse at that moment of the expression on my face, they would have seen my eyes and my future brighten to a level that those flowers could never reach.

*   *   *

After the massage, Crystal and I both received our manicure and pedicure in silence, enjoying the lightness of our bodies and the soothing fountains gurgling around us. We then energetically shuffled in our spa slippers and robe to the drying lamps situated in a private corner. As we settled in, Crystal abruptly broke the silence.

"You know, girl, I've played it out over and over in my head, and I just can't understand the mentality of these low self-esteem trifling home-wreckers who can't find a man of their own so they're willing to have affairs with married men." She shook her head in an expression of her disgust.

"Actually, Crystal, I've heard some women say that they're not the one who's having the affair, he is. And if the wife was on top of her game the way that she should be, then the man wouldn't be looking for someone else to satisfy his needs." As soon as I started, I knew I should have held my tongue, but it was too late. My tone of voice had too much emotion; it may have revealed that I cared, and not necessarily about Crystal.

"You sound like a woman with experience," Crystal peered at me with her inquiring and quizzical look honed over years of being an attorney.

Not wanting to tip my hand, I quickly shook my head and non-chalantly said, "No, it's not like that. I've just been watching a lot of television shows in which the other women express their view-point for why they're seeing a married man. I thought you might want to know what they're saying."

With a sisterly look of displeasure, Crystal instructed me, "Monica, you need to use your time more wisely than watching some damn show about women trying to defend against and jus-tify destroying other people's relationships." Crystal turned back around and readjusted herself in the chair.

"Crystal, you see, that's exactly their point." I was a slightly annoyed by her you-should-know-better tone of voice, but I tried not to let it show. "They say the relationship was already destroyed before they even came into the picture. They're just reaping the rewards and getting in on the ground floor to lock in a man before he becomes single again and hits the open market."

Crystal rolled her eyes and gave me an incredulous look. Then, maintaining a well-rehearsed smile on her face she said, "I can't believe that you're taking their side."

"I'm not taking anyone's side. I was just trying to share with you a different perspective." I shrugged and hoped the conversa-tion would quickly come to a close.

"Well, Monica, I take offense at that. We are more than col-leagues, we're friends, so you are supposed to take sides. Mine."

Whenever Crystal raised her eyebrows like that, I knew it

meant she was starting to become annoyed. "Crystal, you know I got your back," I replied trying to reassure her. "And if it weren't for my wet nails, I'd give you a hug right now. Everything's going to be all right. Don't worry."

My comment apparently softened her a little, and she gave a slight grin. After a few moments of silence, however, Crystal commented, "If I was with DJ, then none of this nonsense that I have to face with Steven would even be going on. I can't stand the fact that that uppity political snake Vanessa is married to him."

"I thought you let that go. That you were over him." Now I really was aggravated. Crystal was acting all high and mighty like she was better than the so called other woman, but she's not innocent herself. She may not be physically cheating on Steven, but emotionally she's long since been having an affair of her own.

"I have let it go. It's just that there are qualities about DJ that if Steven had them, then I wouldn't even be having this conversation with you."

That's it right there. That's why I don't feel guilty about sleeping with your husband, I thought to myself. I couldn't stand hearing Crystal so unfairly compare Steven to DJ. I don't know about DJ and Vanessa, I wanted to tell her, but I know for certain that Steven would be much better off with a woman who was a true partner, someone who wanted to build an empire with him. Someone like me. Instead, I decided to change the subject.

"How is your baby Shelton holding up in light of the murder charges?" I gently inquired.

Crystal sighed heavily. "He's trying to stay strong and keep his head up. But it's hard. People he thought he could count on have turned their back. I knew it would happen."

"It's got to help, though, that he has such a loving and skilled attorney for a mother," I commented trying to play to her large ego.

"You don't have any children, so you can't understand," she began as I locked my jaw into a fixed, yet somewhat strained smile. How dare she patronize me. She continued, "But as a mother there is just such a strong bond with your child. You'd do anything to protect them. Once we get Shelton off these charges, I'm going pursue the real killer with a vengeance so that there's no question of Shelton's innocence."

"How is he dealing with the media?"

"It's been rough. Shelton can hardly come out of the house without being trailed by paparazzi. And even when they aren't pursuing him, it seems that every no-name nobody is trying to capitalize off of our misfortune by snapping cell phone pictures and video to put on the Internet or the latest entertainment news show for the world to see."

"Some people have no consideration for others' feelings," I commented.

"I hope, though," Crystal continued, "that with the upcoming elections and the political scene getting into full gear that our story will be able to fade to the back and the district attorney will be so absorbed with his campaign that there won't be much time left to pursue the indictments."

I also hoped all the campaigning would keep public officials from pursuing their other duties. While Crystal seemed to carefully steer the conversation away from the most recent events in her household, I knew from Steven that Shelton actually moved out of the house and in with DJ. This only compounded Steven's sense of betrayal. My heart went out to him. Not only did Shelton give information to the FBI to implicate Steven, and not only has his wife been secretly trying to change Steven into DJ for years, but now the bastard son Steven had given his legitimate name to was so infatuated with DJ that he wanted to be him.

From my perspective, Shelton was causing more trouble than he was worth. When I told Steven of Shelton's disloyalty in giving information to the authorities, he was definitely saddened and hurt by it, but not destroyed by the news like I thought he would be. Given Steven's response and the fact that Shelton wasn't even his own blood, I set some wheels into motion to put an end to not only the treachery but to Shelton as well. Why should his duplicity put the man I love into prison and tear down everything we've worked for? Crystal was wrong. I do understand the kind of love that will make you do anything to protect your loved ones.

The ringing of Crystal's cell phone abruptly interrupted our conversation and my ruminations. From the ring tone, Crystal knew it was Steven, so she gingerly opened up the phone's flap and answered it.

"Hey there, sweetie," she cooed. "…. Mmm hmm. You know I would love that," she giggled. Crystal then flashed me a huge smile out of apparent excitement over whatever Steven was telling her. I tried not to show any displeasure and smiled back.

"…Well, I'm actually not alone right now... Monica's here, so we'll have to discuss that at home. Tonight." Crystal's tone of voice was almost cryptic, as if she was trying to give Steven some kind of secret message in light of my presence. The widening of her eyes and the huge grin that spread across her face didn't help to diminish my suspicions. What the hell was he saying to her?

After another minute or so, I'd had enough. "My nails are done," I announced loudly with an air of impatience, "and I've got somewhere to go." I hastily stood up. Crystal, still giggling like a school girl, followed suit.

Placing her hand over the phone, she whispered to me, "Husbands…if you get a man, you'll understand."

Miffed, I spun around before Crystal could detect the flash of rage on my face. I wanted to storm off, stomping my feet the whole way like a two-year-old, but instead I mustered all of the Jack-and-Jill poise drilled into me from a young age and genteelly strolled to my changing room. Even through the walls, I could still make out Crystal's flirtatious tone of voice.

I had to hand it to Crystal. She definitely took the manipulative woman stereotype to a different level. It took skill to step out on Steven, become pregnant by another man, and then trap him into marrying you. While I didn't doubt that Steven loved Crystal at the beginning, to me she was just a glorified baby mamma with a wedding ring.

I waited until I heard Crystal say goodbye to Steven before I came out of the dressing room. Having some skill of my own, I gave Crystal a knowing smile as she emerged from her changing room. "Based on that phone call, it sounded to me that things are well in the Calloway household."

"Maybe you're right. Maybe I don't have anything to worry about."

"I am right," I playfully insisted. "From this end, you two sounded like two teenagers in love."

"He was just calling to check in on me." As soon as she finished her comment, Crystal's cell phone rang with that familiar tone once again. I tried not to show any displeasure. Crystal shrugged and then remarked before she answered the phone, "He can be so doting at times."

Chatting away, Crystal followed me to the receptionist's desk to pay for the spa service.

"Massage, manicure, pedicure, our signature lemon exfoliate scrub," the receptionist began ticking off the treatments we had received.

Trying to continue her conversation with Steven while simultaneously wanting to check out the total, Crystal peered over my shoulder as the receptionist and I confirmed the bill.

At that very moment, the newly hired hostess came on duty. Apparently wanting to impress me with her memory, the young woman looked directly at me and gushed, "Mrs. Calloway, it is so good to see you again. You're such a faithful customer. I am glad to see that you're taking advantage of that gift certificate your wonderful husband purchased for you. Was everything as you expected?"

CHAPTER EIGHTEEN

L isten, Jordan. You either wear a wire and cooperate with us, or you and your wife will end up dead or in jail. There is no way around this," threatened the FBI agent.

Stubborn and determined to defend my constitutional rights, I snapped back, "I haven't committed any crimes. Why in the world would I need to wear a wire? You definitely have the wrong person."

"I'm not asking you. I'm telling you. Don't play dumb with me. Do you hear me? There is a lot at stake. You know exactly what I'm talking about. Who sent you to see Bishop Jackson?"

"To my knowledge meeting with a pastor is not a crime." Not pleased by my response, the FBI agent slammed his fist against the metal table shaking it, but not me, as I sat motionless in the windowless, closet-sized room. He then leaned closer to me and growled, "That's not what I asked you, damn it. I asked you, who sent you and who are you representing?"

Silently, I just stared at him without emotion as I fantasized about all the things I would do to him if we were one-on-one versus him having several FBI agents with M-16 automatic rifles standing guard just outside door.

Earlier when the flashing lights pulled me over, I thought it was the standard driving while Black male experience that so many

Black men go through where you are pulled over for no other reason than to falsely accuse and harass you of either committing or on your way to committing a crime.

I even managed to remain calm as three carloads of agents jumped out of their vehicles with guns drawn demanding that I place my car into park and keep my hands on the steering wheel at all times. In light of what has happened to so many other Black men, I was just relieved that flashlight beams shot through the front window versus bullets.

*   *   *

"Jordan, you're an educated man. You have several letters after your name. I'm curious. Do you know what CCE stands for or 21 USC848?" inquired the restless FBI agent in an apparent change in tactics as he leaned backwards in the steel non-cushioned chair.

"CCE?" I repeated.

"Yeah, CCE or 21 USC848. Have you ever come across those terms before?"

"Not that I can recall."

The man snapped his fingers and pointed at me, "Now that makes sense. I believe you, because if you knew that CCE stood for Continued Criminal Enterprise, then you, being the smart man that you are, would want to show me that you did."

"So what's your point?" I asked in a slightly irritable tone.

Resting his elbows on the table and looking me in the eye, he began, "My point is, educated man, that 21 USC848 is a narcotic conspiracy. Matter fact, it says in 21 USC841, and you can quote me that it is unlawful for any person to knowingly and intentionally manufacture, distribute, dispense or possess with the intent to manufacture, distribute, or dispense a controlled substance; or to knowingly and intentionally create, distribute, dispense or possess with the intent to distribute or dispense."

I stared at him blankly and gave a slight shrug that said, "Who cares."

Reacting to my nonchalance, he smiled and said softly, "If this is too much legalese, then I'll make it more plain for you so you'll get it. Any of the offenses that I mentioned under 21 USC841 for which a person is convicted can result in a sentence of life in prison. The offense is considered committed and the law broken merely by the agreement to do the prohibited act, regardless of whether or not the prohibited act was ever or could be completed."

The FBI agent, feeling that he had just laid out some kind of major insight or revelation, leaned forward in his chair in a self-satisfied manner and waited for my response.

After a few brief moments of silence, I replied, "Like I told you before, what the hell does this have to do with me?"

"See, I knew you were going to say that," replied the FBI agent before saying, "Thank you, Jordan, and I do mean thank you. For because of you I just won a $50 bet." He then suddenly yelled out, "I won. I told you he doesn't know anything. Can someone, anyone, bring me manila envelope number one?"

A broad-shouldered, scowl-faced marine type in camouflage fatigues and shiny black combat boots entered the cell-like room and placed the 8-1/2 by 11-inch envelope on the table before us and then quickly exited without saying a word.

Hours ago my watch and cell phone had been removed from

my wrist and inner jacket pocket during a search and frisk even before I entered this quasi-closet. Blindfolded, I had sat cooped up for long stretches of time in this interrogation center without even a sip of water. Since the blindfold had been removed, I had been bombarded by questions seeking to determine the nature of my relationship with Bishop Jackson and which presidential candidate did I finally agree to work with since I had spoken to representatives from both camps.

While I couldn't figure out which answer they wanted to hear, I knew there was no way I was about to begin divulging information about the work I was doing to strategically bring down the Black presidential candidate. Maybe this whole scenario was even a test by the Preachers' Syndicate. I had heard the stories, though I didn't believe them, that the preachers were connected high up in the government and would utilize unconventional means to verify the veracity of those they dealt with.

Regardless, while I couldn't decipher this whole scene, I did know that I was thirsty, hungry and tired of playing their games. So I stared dead into the FBI agent's eyes and demanded in the most authoritative voice I could muster, "I want to be let go or booked. Am I making myself clear? Effective immediately, if you are arresting me, then arrest me and perform your duty of reading me my Miranda rights. I then want to make a phone call to acquire the lawyer of my choice."

He was unfazed by my demands. "Jordan, before we talk about those issues, I want for you, since you did help me win $50, to open up this envelope and tell me what you think."

Annoyed by his one-man good cop/bad cop routine and frustrated by the entire scenario, I pressed my point. "I don't need to open up any envelopes. Get your supervisor. I want to speak to someone who is in charge, because there is a heavy price that someone is going to have to pay if I am not let out of here soon."

In a coaxing manner, the FBI agent looked at the envelope and said, "Aren't you even curious what's in it? He then proceeded to pull out a photo of my wife Theresa shimmering down a stripper's pole with barely anything on.

The next words out of his mouth had something to do with "What a nice rack." I couldn't be certain, because before he could complete his sentence, I lunged towards him over the metal table causing for him to jump backwards.

"Guards," he yelled.

In milliseconds, menacing men with machinegun barrels pointed at my face barked orders for me to remain still or they would kill me without hesitation.

*   *   *

"Okay Jordan, let's try this again. I promise you that after you open the envelope you will be on your way out of here before you know it," smiled the FBI agent.

Determined to prove that there were no secrets between me and my wife, Theresa, I reluctantly decided to demonstrate my point by eagerly embracing whatever existed in the mysterious envelope.

The first couple of promiscuous photos I viewed had Theresa bending over wearing nothing more than a g-string, posing promiscuously on a stripper pole and touching herself in places that as her husband only I saw.

As I flipped through several more photos, I had to constantly remind myself that this Theresa existed long before the college-educated woman whom I had come to know and adore. Even with her determination to rise above her circumstances despite the lack of positive family role models, I knew Theresa had not been unscathed by her environment. But things were different now, and she was different now. I had long ago accepted her past and looked ahead with her to the woman of God she was becoming.

Not seeing the relevance between my detention and semi-naked photos of my wife, I stopped after the fifth photo and said, "What is your point? I've looked at the photos, as you requested, and I don't see how any of them are anywhere near on the level of putting my wife and me in jail, getting us killed or narcotic-related offenses."

"Jordan, are you testing me? Because if you are testing me to see if I believe you, then I have to say I do. Now it doesn't make a difference, but I do. So I'll tell you what. I'm going to help you out. Who do you see in the background of those photos?"

I curiously eyed the FBI agent. It had not even dawned on me to look at anything but Theresa. The people in the background of the photos were just a blur to me, but as I glanced back at the pictures, I had a little better understanding of what caught the FBI's attention. However, this still gave me no insight as to why they wanted me.

"Okay. I see people. Men," I replied as I casually tossed the photographs onto the table and sat back in my chair.

"Now, Jordan, that wasn't cool. I expected more from you. You could have said that you see the Associate Minister of First Central Church having a sexual act performed on him. You know the guy, right? He's the marriage counselor over there? Nasty rumors going around about him. Did he counsel you and Theresa?"

I glared at him trying not to respond to his taunting.

"No? Well, let's try another. You could have said that in this one you saw a prominent political official who's just burst into the political scene toasting champagne glasses with one of the city's most notorious drug dealers and surrounded by a bunch of scantily clad women." He picked up the photograph and examined it closely, commenting, "And I don't think they're his daughters."

Setting that picture aside, he pointed to another one and continued, "Oh, now, you definitely should have gotten this one. Look. There's your real estate investment buddy, a little slimmer, of course, puffing away on a cigar and laughing with some local politicians, maybe even the elected assessor, and some low key drug dealers. I wonder why they were there...."

Before he could pick up another photograph and continue his twisted version of "This Is Your Life," I conceded, "You're right. Maybe I could have looked harder and seen some of things that you saw, but...."

"Do you like music, Jordan?"

"What?"

"Music. You know, notes, rhythm, melody."

"What does music have to do with anything?"

Almost as if on cue, there was a knock at the door, and the same burly G.I. Joe character from before carried in his hand a digital musical player playing *Your Girl, My Ho.*

"Quite a song, huh?" the FBI agent commented as he rhythmically tapped on the table to the beat of the music. "That Prince

Murda guy, he's a trip. My sons love his music, this song especially. I, myself, prefer Killa C. But what do I know?"

"His name isn't Prince Murda. It's Prince Hall."

"Really? That's not what it says on my CD cover…. Your girl,
My Ho," he sang along. "I wonder if anyone's ever called Theresa
that."

"All right," I cut in, exacerbated by his most recent slight
towards my wife. "I've had enough. This makes no damn sense. I
want to see your supervisor now."

The FBI agent casually turned off the music and then responded without any level of detectable attitude, "Okay, Jordan. You
want to see my supervisor, fine. Not that you're in the position to
demand anything, but I'll send someone to get my supervisor. No
problem." The agent motioned to the guard at the door who then
subsequently left the room only to be replaced with another look-
alike. "In the mean time, let's continue to get to know one another. So, how do you know Prince Murda?"

"You already know, I'm quite sure, that he's my brother-in-
law."

"Yes, I do. And did you know that Prince Murda was trying to
get out of his hip-hop contract with Pure Hustla Records, a sub-
sidiary of Calloway Enterprises?" He then pointed back to the
photographs still strewn across the table. "Now I gave you a head
start, so you should get it. Think 'Where's Waldo?' Is there anyone else in the photos that I didn't name or allude to?"

I examined the photos intently even though my eyes were
straining from the dim light in the room. I didn't get it at first, but
after a few seconds, I somewhat understood what the agent was
trying to get me to see. Steven "Make Money" Calloway was in

every single photograph.

"Okay. So I see Steven Calloway. What's your point?"

"My point is, there are those who believe that Prince Murda tried to use these same pictures that I'm showing you for blackmail. In fact, he is reported to have told Mr. Calloway that unless he was let out of his contract, he was going to put the photographs out for public consumption, which, as you can imagine given the number of prominent elected officials present as well as drug dealers and female escorts, would certainly be cause for a scandal and public relations nightmare."

I nodded my head in recognition of the humiliation and uproar such a move would have caused, but I still didn't get how it all connected to me. "I see that, but none of it is any of my business."

"Well, let me tell you what my business is." The FBI agent suddenly lost his air of playfulness and took on a no-nonsense manner. "You have been recruited by one of the major presidential candidates to bribe a group of corrupt preachers. Their influence on how their congregations vote is so powerful that it may determine who will be the next president of the United States in this upcoming election."

"I want to see an attorney right now," I immediately called out. "I have nothing more to say. It is my patriotic right to plead the fifth."

The FBI agent shook his head slowly back and forth as if he were disappointed in my decision to seek counsel. He then let out a deep sigh and leaned forward as though he was going to say something.

Sensing that he wasn't taking my request for access to an attorney serious enough, I didn't wait for his response. Instead, I reiterated, "You have no idea how much trouble you are causing for yourself. Legally, you are on very thin ice. If I were you, I'd find out what's taking so long with your supervisor and let him know that this illegal detention has lasted several hours and is about to become something far worse than he and the FBI could ever imagine."

Given the intensity with which I made my speech as well as the injustice that they were perpetrating against me, laughter was the last response I expected from the man across the table.

The FBI agent then refocused himself and said, "I get it now. Jordan, you have no idea how much trouble you're in. While you think I've crossed some kind of magical ethical or moral line, you have no idea who you are crossing in your dealings with the Preachers' Syndicate. You think I'm FBI. We're not the FBI. This badge number, that I am sure you have memorized, is a fake. An illusion.

"I work for a top secret, classified unit whose name is irrelevant to our discussions. But what is important for you to understand is that this country is at war. The next president of the United States will be making geo-political decisions concerning that global war that will affect billions of people across the world and trillions of dollars. And we'll be damned if those pastors mess up all that we have planned."

My jaw dropped when he said he wasn't FBI. I was caught off guard and was now internally searching for answers. I couldn't even speak.

"Jordan," he added, "normally we wouldn't give a damn about a bunch of corrupt preachers who exchange their influence for sweet land deals, secret bank accounts full of their parishioners' money so they can splurge it on their mistresses, fancy vehicles and whatever else, but this is different. Entire economic markets can change direction based on who the president is. Trade deals. Treaties. The value of the U.S. currency. It all rests on the outcome of the election. That's how big this is. The game is so high stakes that no one is letting this go. And that's where you come in."

He then readjusted himself in the chair before making his next point. "We have bank records, video surveillance and sworn testimony from convicted felons who are trying to reduce their jail term that Theresa Hall knowingly took money from a major drug dealer for several years to pay for her college tuition. She benefited from a criminal enterprise. Later on, the both of you, when you purchased your first home, used money Theresa had received as a gift from her brother Prince Murda who is associated with drug dealers."

"I knew nothing about this."

"It doesn't matter. Your home and several real estate deals that you participated in could not have occurred without the investor who appears in this photo," said my unidentified captor as he used his index finger to point out my partner from my real estate investment club. "Everything that you own and worked to get, from real estate, to cars, businesses, everything is going to be forfeited under USC846." With each item he listed, the man hit his knuckles on the table to drive home the level of what I was facing. "On top of that, we have enough evidence to prosecute you in a secret court where you can't even see the evidence against you. You and your dear wife Theresa will be in jail for over a 100 years, damn near in solitary confinement, in an undisclosed prison facility."

"This is America. You can't do that. I have rights protected by the United States Constitution."

"The Constitution, huh? You're Black, Jordan. I know you know better. Have you forgotten the Native Americans, Indians or whatever you want to call them? Does COINTELPRO mean anything to you? It is history repeating itself with a new spin. Are you not following the news? Have you not seen what is occurring in the name of fighting terrorism across the globe and even at home in the United States? Rights mean nothing. They don't exist. We can do whatever we want, when we want, 'cause we want. And what we want from you is for you to wear a wire."

"I got to think this through."

"There is nothing to think through. The choices are simple. Do you want to live or do you want to die? Do you want to spend the rest of your life in prison or out walking freely on the street? Do you or do you not care if the lives of the people you love the most will all be in danger if you make the wrong choice?"

"How do I even know this is real?"

The man pulled out my cell phone from his pocket and said, "Your mother is currently seated in the back of a town car driven by one of my men under the guise that you planned a special surprise for her that you wanted for her to see. Lovely woman. On my orders, your mother will be killed and her body destroyed in boiling liquid to take care of the remains and dental records. Why don't you give her a call. She thinks she's on her way to meet you right now." He then pressed the preset number for my mother and passed me the phone.

My mother's loving voice picked up the phone and said,

"Sweetie. What surprise do you have for me that requires for you to send a town car to pick me up?"

"A great surprise, Momma," I managed to say while holding my head in one hand and the phone in the other. What had I gotten myself into? And what was I going to do to get out of it? "Are you okay, Momma?"

"Yes, baby. The fine men you sent to pick me up have just been so nice and kind. I'm looking forward to seeing you."

"Me, too."

"I love you."

"I love you, too."

Uncertain of what my next move should be, I hung up the phone, took a deep breath and said, "Now tell me. What exactly do you want for me to do?"

CHAPTER NINETEEN

I don't know if it's God's plan for us to be together for a lifetime or just a time in our life. I just know that whenever you and I are together we have the time of our life," recounted the sincere groom-to-be, Anthony Thompson, about the loving sentiments he had shared with his beautiful fiancée.

I was so proud of both of them. As the pastor of Mount Caramel Baptist Church it was something so nice to see. With all the dysfunctional relationships in this world, they were a refreshing example of the power of God to unite two people into a healthy and God-honoring relationship. Their commitment to one another was a reminder that love was not only real and attainable, but that love, just like us, needed to be loved and cherished. Based upon the seriousness with which they both took their relationship with God, it was no surprise that over time they took their friendship to prayer and found that God had much bigger plans in store for them together.

"Pastor, I want to thank you deeply for agreeing to officiate at my wedding," began Anthony as we alternated practicing putts on the five-star hotel putting green located against the backdrop of the Caribbean Sea's turquoise-blue water. He then turned to me and said, "I recognize you're very busy and have a lot on your plate. It means a lot to me that you would take time out of your schedule. You've been such a positive and powerful force in my life."

Playfully, I said, "You've got it all twisted. I'm the one who needs to be thanking you. Look at this." I spread out my arms as if to encompass the expansive beauty of the PGA championship golf course. "It doesn't get much better. And with all that has been going on in my life, getting away for a couple of days to play some golf and lay around in the sun was exactly what I needed."

The fact is, I had been in need of a vacation, of some time away, for quite a while. The most recent controversies I've become embroiled in certainly hadn't been the first. When my father was still alive and I was the new associate minister for men at Mount Caramel, an unarmed Black man who lived in the local community had been shot repeatedly and killed by several police in what they said was an act of self-defense. As their case unraveled, the cover-up thickened, and the mayor's office had made it known to many of the local pastors that any future access to his office, and subsequently to grant funds, would rest on how hard one pressed on this issue.

I reminded my father and others that as a strong Black Christian man I had grown to understand that there are times when God wants for you to stand still and other times God wants for you to still stand no matter what the consequences that the world may threaten. The killing of an unarmed Black man could not just be prayed away or forgotten as part of yesterday's news. It had to be dealt with through Christian love seeking justice.

It was during those press conferences, prayer breakfasts, high school graduations, city council meetings, community meetings and radio interviews that Anthony Thompson and I came to get to know each other better. We both understood the importance of being men with integrity and purpose.

Switching golf clubs to prepare for a 15-foot putt, I added to my earlier comments by saying, "On a serious note, having masculine, intelligent, take-no-nonsense, Bible-knowing, strong men of God like yourself at Mount Caramel is something that needs to be promoted and supported. We're fortunate to have you as a part of the fellowship and especially leading the young men's mentoring program."

"Thank you, Pastor. That means a lot," Anthony said as he gave me the universal Black man handshake. Anthony then motioned towards a gentleman walking in our direction past the palm trees swaying in the gentle breeze.

"That brother right there is my closest friend in the entire world. We have been friends since childhood. As far as I'm concerned, he is family, and I would give my life for him." As the immaculately dressed brother approached, the groom-to-be gave him a big grizzly bear hug and introduced us by saying, "This is my main man, Courtland. He's going to be the best man in my wedding."

The power of these two men bonding together impressed me. Since becoming the pastor of Mount Caramel Baptist Church, I had placed a high priority on reaching out to men both in the congregation and in the general community as a whole. Despite being the son of a preacher, I understood personally why so many men don't come to church. They were turned off by all the pimps sitting up in the pulpit who were more interested in using people, especially women, for their own gratification and gain rather than sharing the gospel.

177

Large numbers of Black men felt excluded or didn't see how the biblically watered-down message that many preacher's preach spoke to the conditions in their lives and the challenges that they faced, let alone how it was relevant to the political and socio-economic realities of the world. God had charged me to preach the gospel of Jesus Christ as Lord and Savior in season and out of season to all who would hear irrespective of race, gender, income, or other variables. Sharing the Word of God to men and watching them empower themselves and others with the love, strength, purpose and conviction that comes from a having a personal relationship with Jesus was one of the few times in life that I could truly say that I was at peace.

Courtland, Anthony and I began packing up the golf cart for our tee time on the front nine. As Anthony drove us to the first hole, he turned slightly toward me as I sat in the back and said, "Pastor, I told my man Courtland that I wanted for y'all to meet person-to-person because I really felt that y'all could vibe together."

Courtland, not one accustomed to hiding his perspective or opinion, looked me straight in the eye and said, "I'm not going to lie to you. I'm not really into church."

"I'm not either," I quickly responded back, which caught him totally off guard. I could tell by the bewildered look on his face that he wasn't expecting me to say that to him. I then clarified my comment by saying, "I'm into Christ, not church. We are saved and redeemed by Jesus Christ, not the church. The church is a building, which can be filled with people who are about something or people who aren't or a combination of the two." I then added, "Don't misinterpret what I'm saying to mean that the church doesn't have a vital role to play, because it definitely does, depending on what is being preached and taught in that church about Jesus Christ. There are a lot of places that call themselves a church but don't teach the truth and power about Jesus and His Holy Word. Some churches are just a meeting place for religious people versus a place of fellowship for people who are trying to live a life pleasing to Jesus Christ as Lord and Savior."

Anthony interjected into the conversation. "I told you, Courtland, that both of you were going to see eye-to-eye on some things."

Courtland nodded his head and said, "No doubt. No doubt."

Having arrived at the first hole, we selected our drivers and began taking turns teeing off. Courtland's long drive let me know he would be a fierce competitor. Based on our earlier conversation, I took the opportunity to invite him to Mount Caramel and especially to our men's Bible study.

As we traveled to the next hole on the golf course, Courtland responded to my invitation. "It sounds interesting, and I'm definitely intrigued, but to be real with you, I'm not convinced that reading a book by a bunch of dead people who lived thousands of years ago is going to help me with my real life circumstances. While I'm not the only one, I have major things and decisions to deal with. So what does reading the Bible have to do with today?" As I paused to gather my thoughts in response, Courtland quickly added in, "I'm not trying to be disrespectful. I'm just trying to be real with you since you've been real with me."

Anthony then, in a joking way, chimed in, "Pastor will have his own answer, but like I told you before, you need cut all those women you messing around with, Courtland. Those women done got my main man all confused. I told you before that your life as a playa was played out. You need to find one good woman who's in your corner who loves the Lord and take your relationship to prayer to seek God's purpose, and if God gives you the green light, then stick with her."

Immediately we all started to laugh. After a few more jokes between the two best friends, Courtland then turned the conversation back to a more serious tone and said to me as we waited for the golfers ahead of us to finish the hole, "I really would like for you to answer me, because that is something that I've thought about. I just haven't had the opportunity to pursue my question in a format or forum where I felt comfortable."

I knew that the next thing I said was going to be especially important to Courtland. As I reached back and passed them each a bottled water from the cooler, I also took a deep breath while simultaneously praying to God that God would reveal to me something to share with this brother that would touch his heart and his circumstances. By the time I exhaled, God had answered my prayer.

"Courtland," I began, "one of the best discussions we had during our men's Bible study was when we were talking about our experiences of betrayal. For each of us, the dark pain of betrayal had occurred either in our personal relationships or with family members, in job experiences as well as what we all see in the world at large."

I then said, "The biblical text that we studied dealt with Judas and his betrayal of Jesus. In the book of Mark, Chapter 14, verses 43 through 47, it says, 'And immediately while Jesus was still speaking, behold Judas, one of the twelve disciples along with chief priest, scribes and elders and soldiers carrying swords and clubs approached Him. Now Jesus' betrayer, which is Judas, had given them a sign saying, whomever I kiss. He is the One: seize Him. Immediately Judas went up to Jesus and said, "Greetings, Rabbi!" And kissed Him and they seized Jesus him.' "

Courtland respectfully and attentively listened to everything I said and then commented, "It's interesting that you bring up betrayal. Before you continue, I want to bring to your knowledge what just recently happened. There's this woman who I've been dealing with heavily as of late. I even told her I loved her."

"I haven't heard this one," Anthony remarked. "Is that the chick you met at the reception?"

"Yeah," Courtland replied. "But get this. When I was recently out of town on business, I let her stay at my place because she told me that she was studying hard for the Bar exam and needed to get away from her noisy law school roommate."

"Bad move, man," Anthony observed as he shook his head. "It was too early to let a woman have access to your crib like that."

"I definitely see that now, but at the time I was wanting to be supportive, so I was cool with all that. It turns out, however, that she was really fooling around with her law school roommate's man behind both of our backs."

"Ooh," Anthony and I exclaimed in unison at the mere thought of the pain that must have caused.

"Exactly. She had decided to use my townhouse as the secret rendezvous spot for her and the guy to get together sexually while I was out of town. This was at my house, mind you. I don't think I can say it enough. This occurred at my house."

Anthony and I remained respectfully silent, almost as if we

were honoring the dead, as the three of us walked together to the putting green. I was just about to say something when Courtland continued, "And that ain't it. I just found out that a guy at my job that I've being going to lunch with on a regular basis and who has worked closely with me on numerous projects, recently stole a key campaign legislative proposal off my computer that I had been laboring over and sold that information to a rival candidate that he is now going to work for."

Stopping and leaning on his golf club for effect, Courtland challenged, "Now if you can relate that Scripture you told me to my experiences, then when we get back to the states, I'm going make my way to your men's Bible study."

Anthony flashed me a look that said, "Pastor, don't let us down. I've been talking you up." Earlier, Anthony had told me privately that he had invited a large number of guys that he knew from his college days, neighborhood, and family to come out for a weekend bachelor party in the Caribbean. He expected that a whole lot of men were going to show and eventually he could use his wedding and the events leading up to it as an opportunity to share the gospel of Jesus Christ with people he loved. This was one of those opportunities to do just that.

"Courtland, there is a whole lot you will benefit from by personally studying the Bible, because there really is nothing new under the sun. In regards to the Scripture concerning Judas's betrayal of Jesus, I will give three key points—you know preachers always have to have their three points," I joked, "—and then we can it discuss more later."

"Cool," Courtland replied, focusing in on my words in the midst of the peace and tranquility surrounding us.

"Point number one is this: Remember that when Judas approached Jesus to betray Jesus, he kissed Jesus. It is a kiss that normally took place on the cheek. Nothing homosexual about it. It was a form of greeting in their time. This point that I'm going to make I am sure you can relate to. Remember, everybody that kisses on you ain't in love with you. Sometimes they have a secret agenda, and that secret agenda is about destroying and using you versus loving and protecting you.

"The kiss is just a tool to make you put your guard down so they can set you up in order to bring you down. Be careful who you let get so close to you that they feel comfortable giving you a kiss. And for some people, you don't need their kiss, you need to tell them, 'Kiss off.' Did you get that one, Courtland?"

"I hear you," he replied as he nodded and contemplated what I had shared. "That definitely hits."

Anthony gave me a knowing glance to indicate that I was reaching his friend.

As we each took turns hitting at the next hole, I continued to expound upon the Holy Word of God. "So here's point two, and you tell me how well this relates to what you shared." I squared up to the tee and lined up my swing as I continued to say, "Judas was one of the disciples. He had access to Jesus and even hung around Jesus. They would go places together and do things together. Judas would be on many occasions right by Jesus' side. And this is the biblical key." I reached back with my club and hit the ball with such power and accuracy, I even surprised myself.

The two men nodded with approval, "Not bad."

"If you like that, then check this out," I continued as I placed the driver back into my bag. "The key is, not everybody who is by your side is necessarily on your side. You got to be careful whom you have around in your inner circle. Just because somebody is constantly around you doesn't mean that they are there for you. The reason some people are around you is sometimes so that they can be in the best position to betray you when the price is right."

"I hear you," Courtland confirmed.

"Not everybody is happy to see you succeed. Get that promotion. Develop that healthy, Christian-based relationship that is pleasing to God. Not everyone is happy when you are moving forward in life towards God's purpose that God has for you. You need to be about positive things and keep positive people by your side and remember that lurking sometimes in the crowd may be someone who is by your side but not necessarily on your side."

"And that's exactly what happened with that cat on my job." Courtland shook his head as he thought about his coworker's duplicity. "So you're two for two. What else you got?"

"Keeping score, huh? I like that. And if my math is correct, I got the low score on the holes we've played so far," I bragged.

"Not for long," Anthony warned and took an incredible swing that landed a hole in one.

I let out a long whistle to show that I was majorly impressed. "Have you been taking lessons?" I teased.

"The last point is actually being demonstrated by your friend here," I continued as we got back into the cart to go check out that phenomenal hit. "He just went from dead last to first with one shot. You see, nobody is immune from betrayal. If there is someone out there who would betray Jesus, who never did anybody wrong, then there is someone who most likely at some timeframe or at multiple times in your life is going to betray you. And just as they wanted to seize Jesus in order to bring about Jesus' destruction and death, so there are people who will seek your destruction and death.

"Jesus, as you know, is then falsely persecuted. Convicted. Hung on a cross and dies. But praise God that that is not the end of Jesus' story. And Courtland, I want for you to know that when you have given your life to Jesus Christ as Lord and Savior, then what has happened to you is not the end of your story. Just as Jesus was resurrected and lives, God will raise you out of whatever level of situation you face in order that you might claim the victory. Jesus was one type of victory over betrayal. Yours will be another type of victory over betrayal. But bottom line, you will live because most importantly Jesus lives.

"How'd I do?" I asked the two men with a big grin on my face. I knew I had hit it.

Courtland began nodding approvingly. "Very impressive. Really. I've never heard the Bible explained that way. It's never made sense to me like that before. The Bible has always been some distant text, but you really brought it home."

"So, we'll see you at the next men's Bible study?"

"Oh, most definitely. And if you keep throwin' down like that, I may even show up for Sunday."

Anthony cracked up at Courtland's last comment and comical facial expressions. "I tell ya, Doc. If he does show up, you will have accomplished a great feat. I've been trying to get him to come to church with me for years."

"It was never the right time," Courtland tried to shrug off his friend's comment. "Now may be the right time."

"I just can't wait 'til the rest of the guys show up," Anthony

185

exclaimed. "Because if you can give a wedding sermon like the way you just laid out that learning, there's no telling who'll be saved this weekend. This is awesome."

With a very satisfied, pleased, and yet humble smile, all I could say in reply was "Bless God," because I knew that what I had just shared had nothing to do with me and everything to do with what God wanted to accomplish in Courtland's life. I was merely the conduit, the instrument.

As we continued to talk and share from our experiences of betrayal, the unexpected ringing of my cell phone broke the flow of our blessed fellowship. I didn't even want to check the caller ID let alone answer the phone, but as a pastor, you never know what emergency may require your specialized attention. I flipped open the phone to get a full look at the number, but I didn't recognize it. It wasn't even from the same area code as home.

"Hello?" I answered the phone as I slid off to the side to speak more privately.

"Pastor Goodwell?" the sweet voice asked.

"Yes. May I help you?" My tone was all business.

"Pastor, this is Attorney De'Borah Harriston. I'm so sorry to disturb you."

"De'Borah," my voice brightened remembering the magnificent blessing of her singing during the recent celebration of my anniversary at Mount Caramel, "I didn't recognize your voice without it going two, three, four octaves up. You have an amazing gift. What can I do for you?"

"Actually, Pastor, I'm calling on behalf of my client, your nephew, Shelton Calloway. I don't know if his mother has told, but the family has retained my services in order to legally represent

Shelton regarding the charges that are being brought against him."

"I didn't realize that you were the one representing him. But I've heard wonderful things about your experience and skills."

"Thank you for that encouragement. I am currently working very hard on his defense in the event that the district attorney decides to take it to a grand jury for an indictment. The evidence, as you know, is all circumstantial, so I can't imagine that he would actually move forward on this, but it is an election year and he is running for Congress."

"Yes, it is. It seems it being an election year makes a lot of people do what they normally otherwise wouldn't."

"As I'm preparing for a possible trial, Pastor, it would be very beneficial if we had an opportunity to talk privately in person. There are some questions I would like to ask you."

"Of course. I want to be helpful in any way possible. I believe in my nephew's innocence and I'm committed to do anything I can to clear him of the charges. De'Borah, I'm actually currently out of town officiating at a wedding. Once I return home, I'll give you a call so that we can set up a time. Is this the best number to reach you on?"

"Yes, it is, Pastor. I really appreciate your support and time."

"You're welcome. Have a good day, and give Crystal my best."

As I hung up the phone, I took a deep breath and sighed as reality sunk back in. The lack of clouds in the clear blue Caribbean sky had made me temporarily forget the storms raging in my life—some I knew about and some I hadn't even realized existed.

Stopping to look out over the ocean before I returned to my

golf partners, my thoughts drifted back to Crystal like a raft gently pushed against the shore by the waves. Shelton's recent revelations about my father and Crystal had rocked me, and I wondered if I should say something to her...to let her know that I care, that I support her, and that I'm sorry.

Life would have been so much different. Some things I would have gained, and some things I would have lost. At that moment, my beautiful, intelligent, yet manipulative wife's face flashed in my mind. Vanessa. I wished we would have had the premarital counseling I had given to this couple. Maybe it would have made a difference in us getting married or not. Right now it definitely looks like we're unequally yoked.

As I closed my eyes, I felt the warm Caribbean breeze reminding me of a wonderful time that Crystal and I had had years ago in college. In light of all that had transpired in our lives, I had a deep unspoken desire to tell her, "If I had known that that day was going to be the last day I would ever hold you in my arms, then I would have done everything I could to make that day last forever, so that this day would have never come."

CHAPTER TWENTY

F or the life of me, I can't understand what the Reverend Goodwell ever saw in you," ridiculed a frustrated Trustee Howard during a contentious argument with Vanessa Ford-Goodwell.

"What my husband sees in me is my business. You need to be worried about your own relationship, or lack there of," sneered Vanessa as Trustee Howard paced the white marble floor of his luxury, downtown duplex condo.

"Who said anything about DJ?" asked Trustee Howard with disdain, turning to face her. "I'm talking about the Honorable Reverend Cecil Goodwell—the man who built Mount Caramel Baptist Church into such a major political and economic machine that every politician and business leader in the city would come knocking just to get his opinion and blessing."

"Reminiscing again, I see," retorted Vanessa, dismissing Trustee Howard's grandiose description.

"Look here, Vanessa. You need to show more respect," he chastised. "You ain't never seen a preacher sing nor hoop a congregation into a frenzy the way that Reverend Goodwell did. Your husband DJ is so busy trying to teach, he done put half the congregation to sleep."

Taking a seat and making herself comfortable on the fine

leather couch, Vanessa remarked casually, "I know that you did-n't call a meeting in order to discuss the Reverend Doctor David Josiah Goodwell's preaching technique, now did you?"

"You need to tell him that tithes and offerings have gone down since he sat down the minister of music, Reverend Walker," Trustee Howard directed as he sat in the overstuffed chair across from her.

Tilting her head innocently to the side, Vanessa replied in a sweet tone, "I'm going to leave that source of news to you as the trustee of finance. I don't want to encroach on your territory."

'Very tactfully spoken, Vanessa," Trustee Howard observed. "But I don't believe a word of what you said. You don't want to be the bearer of bad news. That's all."

"Well, you know what they say about killing the messenger." Vanessa gave him a knowing smile.

"Okay. Let's talk serious business." Trustee Howard leaned forward resting his hands on his knees. "Where are we at with the campaign? People are starting to get a little nervous that you can't pull the necessary numbers from the different key constituencies that you need in order to win."

"Where are you getting your numbers from?" asked Vanessa defensively. "According to my campaign manager and senior pollster, I am winning the election."

"I don't know who they're speaking to or calling on the phone, because the numbers that I have seen say that it is a three-way race and that your negative numbers are rising daily."

"It is not my negative numbers that are bringing me down, it's DJ's numbers." Dismayed, Vanessa began rubbing her forehead.

"So have you spoken to him? There is a lot on the line with this election, from control of Congress to determining who the next president of the United States will be."

"I'm doing the best that I can," snapped Vanessa as she arose suddenly and walked towards the picture window that overlooked the downtown skyline, "but he has been so set in his positions and refuses to budge."

"You must be poor in bed. 'Cause if you were any good sexually, he wouldn't be telling you no. He would be doing whatever you told him to so he could hear you say, 'Yes. Yes. Yes.'"

Returning to the couch with an extra sway in her hips, Vanessa scoffed, "Your old behind wishes you could find out how great, not just good, I am in bed. You fantasize about me, don't you?" she cooed as she sat down and crossed her legs showing off her well-formed calf muscles. "You can tell me. I won't tell anybody."

"No," Trustee Howard chuckled. "What I fantasize about are the days when you were never here. When DJ wasn't here. When the Honorable Reverend Cecil Douglass was alive and so powerful in this city that with some well-placed phone calls he almost single-handedly could get almost any person elected after a power lunch and a couple rounds of golf." He shook his head at the memory of such influence.

"Well, I got a news flash for you," Vanessa replied, unaffected. "Reverend Cecil Douglass Goodwell is dead."

Looking her straight in the eye, Trustee Howard spoke deliberately. "And so might a whole lot of other people if we don't find a way for you to win this election and get DJ to support the slate of candidates endorsed by the Preachers' Syndicate."

"That is going to be tough to accomplish." Vanessa sighed deeply. "DJ has not responded well to me. I haven't been able to get him to remove the suspension of Reverend Walker, despite the music minister's popularity and all the e-mails that the church has received from parishioners and people in general."

At a loss, Trustee Howard threw up his arms. "Once again, for the life of me, I can't figure out why Reverend Goodwell thought you coming to Mount Caramel was a step forward."

Offended, Vanessa sucked her teeth, carefully eyed the Trustee, and then stated with confidence, "You can downplay me all you want, but I'm a great asset to this church." Pointing towards the picture window, she continued, "This neighborhood is going through a major re-gentrification, and Reverend Goodwell understood that if the new state senator seat was going to be held by someone who held his best interest in mind, then he needed to have someone who could appeal to various constituency groups that were not only Black or civil rights affiliated."

"Well," mused Trustee Howard in a mocking tone, "if you represent all of that which you describe, then how do you account for why you're not doing better in the polls?"

"Unforeseen circumstances is the best way to put it."

"Hogwash." Trustee Howard abruptly sat back in his chair dismissing Vanessa. "Every political campaign has unforeseen circumstances. Why would you expect that yours would be any different?"

"For the record, unforeseen circumstances are when a person you didn't expect to run against you enters the race. Having your husband's nephew arrested for the murder of a popular video vixen who's in the middle of a hip-hop war and then having newspaper and television shows reporting that the nephew may not actually be your husband's nephew but his illegitimate child are not what I call your traditional circumstances. And to top that off, the damn child is living with us."

"So kick him out the house," Trustee Howard yelled impatiently. "Tell him to pack his bags and go home. His parents have a sprawling mansion for him to go back to. It's not like he will be homeless."

Vanessa stood up once again, this time folding her arms and approaching a wall with a collection of Impressionists' paintings. "I wish it was that simple. DJ, for reasons that I cannot comprehend, is beyond attached to this kid."

"How about the fact that you can't have kids of your own?"

Vanessa glared in response to his question.

"If you knew you couldn't have kids, you should have told someone. How do you expect for us to carry on the Goodwell name?"

"First of all," Vanessa spun around leaving the artwork behind, "I didn't know it was 'us' carrying on the Goodwell name. I'm the only one married to DJ, not you or anybody else. And the last time I checked, your last name was Howard."

"You're damn real my last name is Howard," the Trustee emphatically pointed his finger at Vanessa, "and you better understand that Goodwell is not a last name. It's a brand, and I and Cecil built that brand together into a successful business."

"Pardon me," Vanessa scoffed. "I may be new to the inner workings of a church, but I thought the brand name was Mount Caramel Baptist Church."

"See, you got it wrong." Trustee Howard waved his hand dismissively. "There are lots of churches. A lot of people are preaching about god, prosperity and sprinkling in the name of Jesus in between promoting self-esteem messages that encourage people to believe they can achieve untold riches. We do that, too, but that is not what makes us special. It is not even that Reverend Goodwell used to preach sermons that made everyone feel like they were included and could remain unchanged and stay the way they are. The message was, whatever they preferred, God would still love them."

"Then what is it that you're selling?" Vanessa looked at him intently, genuinely wanting to know the answer.

Picking up on her interest, Trustee Howard leaned in. "We are selling the Goodwell Experience. From the choir to the majestic church edifice, to all the property that the church owns, the DVDs, the TV shows and all the conferences that we put on, the number one thing we promote is the Goodwell Experience. Don't forget that," he emphasized. "That is our edge. People come to see and take part in the Goodwell Experience." Then, in a self-congratulatory manner, he said, "It was a genius marketing ploy."

"Well, you now have answered part of the reason why Reverend Goodwell brought me here." Trustee Howard looked at Vanessa curiously. "I specialize in marketing and have a well-documented history of connecting people and causes together. I am a coalition builder who knows business. And I *love* making money."

Smiling at Vanessa appreciatively, Trustee Howard explained, "Well, the first step to making money in this business is to remember that we are a business that runs as a church, not a church that does business."

Amused, Vanessa asked, "Now that you know I share your love for money you all of a sudden want to be best of friends and give me pointers on how Mount Caramel will help me make money?"

They both chuckled.

"No offense, Vanessa, but when Reverend Goodwell asked his son DJ to come here, it was under the impression that DJ would be a good way to shore up the future of the brand name, especially in light of DJ's success in business and popularity growing up in the community. Now look what we got." Trustee Howard commented incredulously.

"Trustee Howard, I didn't know it myself," confessed a bewildered Vanessa. "I didn't know he actually believed the things that he told me. I thought he was just getting into role playing. Preparing himself for when he actually got here. I didn't know he actually believed that Jesus Christ is Lord and Savior. And when I say he believes, I mean exactly that. He believes it as a fact."

"I thought it was an act, too, but I started noticing over time that the conversations DJ was having with his father were starting to have an impact on business. It wasn't sudden, though. It was a gradual change in certain things."

"Such as?"

"I guess one of the first changes," the trustee began, thinking back, "was that when Reverend Goodwell had a packed house, he used to always make sure he got the offering plate around a couple of extra times so he could get all the money that he could from every visitor. We used to make a killing during the days when people who never come to church came, like during Christmas, New Year's Eve, Mother's Day and the grand daddy of them all, Easter. All of a sudden, he wanted to give the money back into ministries versus buying more church property. I still don't get it."

"Well, I'll tell you one thing. You still can't get a seat in church during Easter."

"And even if you do, you can't see anything with all those big doggone hats," Trustee Howard added.

"So, what to you was the biggest sign that Reverend Goodwell was having a change of heart about the way that y'all ran the business?"

"I can sum it all up in three words: Sin, Hell and Justice."

Intrigued, Vanessa encouraged him to continue. "Explain more about what you mean."

"Reverend Goodwell almost never preached about sin. He might have alluded to the fact they we are all sinners, but he almost never spent time during his sermons detailing the specifics of the types of sins that people were committing, especially when it dealt with lifestyle issues."

Vanessa nodded. "Are you talking about homosexuality? 'Cause DJ and I have had it out several times about his sermons concerning homosexuality and the fact that his sermons are tearing the church apart."

"Exactly. Reverend Goodwell understood that the gay population is very active in our church and did not want to hear sermons criticizing their lifestyle choices. It wasn't good for money."

"So what happened?"

"DJ happened. That's what happened. In their private Bible study sessions, which Reverend Goodwell initially agreed to participate in as a means of indoctrinating DJ into the ways of Mount Caramel Baptist Church, Reverend Goodwell came out a changed man, himself, instead."

Vanessa shook her head in disappointment. "So did you talk to him about it?"

"Of course, and he would go back to what he used to do. But

every once in a while you would hear about sin in a sermon. Then bam." Trustee Howard slammed his hand against a coffee table. "All of a sudden almost every sermon became, 'Repent for the kingdom of God is near.' " Trustee Howard shook his head in disbelief. "Reverend Goodwell started preaching about fornication, gay lifestyle, pride, greed, corruption, you name it."

"What was he saying about Hell?"

"That was my point to him when I heard him preach a sermon about there is a Heaven to gain and a Hell to shun. I was like, what the hell are you doing? Everybody believes that if they go to church they're going to Heaven. That's what keeps them coming. That is why so many people, who never open up a Bible the rest of the week, show up on Sunday. So why are you now preaching to people in church about avoiding going to Hell?"

"And you blame DJ for all this?" Vanessa was deep in thought trying to take in all of what Trustee Howard was sharing so that she could better strategize her next moves.

"That's what it looked like to me. The closer they grew, the more things weren't running the way they were supposed to." After a brief moment to gather his thoughts, Trustee Howard continued. "Now this is probably what, on a personal level, bothered me the most. Reverend Goodwell knew that we had connections and dealings with all types of people. He then out of the blue started talking about corruption and justice and doing what is right biblically and by God. So I was once again up in his office saying, what the hell are you doing? You're putting a lot of people in jeopardy of being prosecuted or exposed as evil people, and they're not going to tolerate it. Especially when they give money to this church as a way to have their sins overlooked."

"And how did he respond?"

"Basically, he didn't. He said he was doing what, as a Christian, God had convicted his heart to do, and that was that. I'm mean, come on. The man hadn't cared about what was right before."

"That is exactly what I'm dealing with now with DJ. He is so caught up in doing what Jesus would want for him to do that he doesn't consider the consequences for himself or me."

"So what are we going to do about this?"

"Well, I don't want what happened to Reverend Goodwell to happen to DJ."

"DJ is too young to have a heart attack." Trustee Howard quickly dismissed the possibility. "He looks like he takes care of himself, works out on a regular basis, and I hear he can still play a pretty mean game of basketball. He has nothing to worry about."

"It's not the heart attack that I'm concerned about. I'm worried about the breaks on his car giving out, not his heart, if you know what I mean."

"I had nothing to do with that. Believe me. If I had known that things had reached a level where people might actually try to kill him, I would have done everything that I could to help avoid it. Reverend Goodwell was like a brother to me. I would have tried to convince them that he could have been worked with. But the Preachers' Syndicate just believed that he was too great of a liability. So there was nothing anyone could do. It tears me apart that he's dead and his son is now placing at risk everything that he built."

"We have got to work more closely together and keep each other better informed of what we know if we are to win this election and continue this family business," Vanessa declared."

"Now we are definitely seeing things the same way. Now I see that the former Reverend Goodwell was right about you." Trustee Howard smiled warmly at Vanessa.

The buzzing of Vanessa's BlackBerry caught her attention. She briefly glanced at the screen and then turned back to Trustee Howard. In a manner that was all business, Vanessa said matter of factly, "Right now, what is most important is that we are both right about one thing. DJ has got to be stopped."

CHAPTER TWENTY-ONE

I'm not killing the kid, regardless of what anyone says. Do you hear me?" I shouted through the cell phone at the principal owner of the G-spot Strip Club. "Shelton may not be my kid, but I don't kill kids…no matter what anyone says."

I had made a lot of bad choices and poor decisions in my life, but even as drunk as I was, I knew better than to kill Shelton. It wasn't his fault that he had gotten entangled in adult situations and drama. Shelton was just an angry teenager who was trying to get back at me as his father for cheating on his moms. He had somehow overheard or come across information, as kids sometimes do, and out of an emotionally vulnerable place had decided to get some revenge for his mother by trying to get me out of the house and out of their lives. At least that is what I believed.

For the last fifteen minutes, I had been sitting in my pimped out SUV with the latest and greatest electronic gadgets, waiting across the street from the office tower where Attorney De'Borah Harriston's firm was located and where Crystal and Shelton had a meeting in the next few minutes. If there were any secret deals on the table with federal and state prosecutors that I didn't know about that would give leniency to Shelton for pleading guilty for killing Evelyn James in exchange for testifying in any upcoming drug or money laundering conspiracy trials, then I wanted to know about it and warn Shelton of the consequences if he should choose to go in that direction. Consequences that I had no control over, even if I did not want to be a part of them.

Shelton was in the adult world, whether it was his choice or not. If he decided to cooperate with the prosecutors, I didn't want Shelton's death on my conscience. He had to be warned of the risk and then make his own decision on what to do next. It was a difficult part of manhood.

I also needed to share with him other things that he didn't know. Shelton needed to know the truth about his mother having been pregnant before we got married as well as that Crystal was not the angelic person that he thought that she was. Our marriage was a fraud. My cheating on Crystal since we were legally married may not have been right, but it certainly should be understandable.

I wanted to remind him of some of the great times we had had before I discovered that he wasn't my kid. My unspoken reaction to him and his mother may not have been the right one, was what I wanted to explain, but it definitely should fall into the category of reasonable versus totally unacceptable. I thought Shelton should also know that I tried to make it work. I just wasn't in a place to get past what Crystal had done in light of all that I had sacrificed, including family, in order to be with her.

Checking my diamond encrusted Rolex watch, I said to myself, "They should have arrived at Attorney Harriston's office by now." They were five minutes late. I sat in total silence. The constant going back and forth of the windshield wipers was the only noise I listened to except for the rhythmic beat of the rain repeatedly hitting the car and asphalt streets. Occasionally a car horn and the whistling of the wind would join in with the sounds made by the rain and start their own impromptu jazz trio.

In life, I had wanted it all, only to find out that it might cost me all that I had. The saddest part of it all was that when it was all said and done, so far I had ended up with nothing worthwhile despite having spent almost all that I had to get it. All throughout my house, located in almost every room from the closets, the kitchen, living room and especially the finished basement, I had purchased everything that you could buy to make one happy only to find that you can't buy happiness.

As of late, the only steady company that I've had was a liquor bottle and gambling habit. Both were addictive. Due to a resilience not of my own, I had not graduated to other forms of narcotics, but the habits I did have were dangerous enough. I clearly understood the cravings and temptations of people who fight different forms of addictions and then, when a crisis comes, find themselves seeking the temporary and dangerous feelings that come from getting high. Every day was a struggle.

A car similar to the one I bought Crystal pulled up, but it wasn't them. As I began to reminisce on both better days and troubling times, I looked towards Heaven and said, "God forgive me of my sins."

*   *   *

You always hear people say, "Once you have kids, your life will never be the same again," and they're right, but I quickly found out that fatherhood meant so much to me that I didn't care that my life had changed. At least not at first.

Holding Shelton as a premature newborn was an amazing

experience. I had spent many months anticipating what he'd look like, what his life would be like, who he would become. And when he arrived, I was so overcome with love. I had no idea where the feeling had come from because the kid sure didn't do anything to earn it. All he did was be born. Yet, I had an intense desire to protect and provide for him. And while I didn't know how I would ever be able to live up to all that he needed me to be, I made up my mind right there and then that no matter what it took, I was going to try to make it happen.

When Shelton was a baby, every new act was thrilling. "Look, his first smile." "Did you see that? He held on to the rattle." And then, he started to talk.

Sitting in my car, I smiled to myself as I thought about the times Shelton said, "Daddy." One in particular that stood out was when we were at the park playing on the swings. I was pushing him from the front so that I could see his sparkling smile and joy-filled giggle. At some point, Crystal called to me so that I could get Shelton's bottle from her. Since the picnic table was at most 15 feet away, I quickly got the bottle and then returned to my son. Shelton greeted me by reaching out his arms and crying out with a huge smile on his face, "Daddy!" I loved that kid, and I loved the feeling of being "Daddy!" Having grown up as the unofficial outcast of my family and under the shadow a brother like DJ who thought he owned the town with his athletic skills and good looks, it was satisfying and felt like vindication to now have a family of my own.

As happy as I was then, I never could have imagined how miserable I would be the day that I learned that Shelton was not actually my son. That night it had been overcast and begun to rain, much like it was doing now. While I was not the athletic type, my son excelled in all forms of sports, and I diligently attended every game I could get to, even adjusting my travel schedule to accommodate his seasons. One particular February evening when Shelton was 11, his basketball team traveled via the school bus to an away game in another county. After the 35 to 33 win in which my son made the game-winning shot, I followed the bus home and began concocting all sorts of plans for how we could celebrate that weekend. Part-way home, as the rain began to fall, the bus driver misjudged his speed, the hairpin turn, and the slick road conditions causing for the bus to flip on its side before my very eyes. Three boys died instantly. Shelton, along with two others, had severe injuries and had to be evacuated via helicopter. I could still conjure up the feeling of helplessness that gripped me that night as I watched his motionless body being placed on the gurney.

Once we arrived at the hospital, I called Crystal and then met with the doctor. He was hopeful about Shelton's condition but said that he had lost a lot of blood and the hospital was running low in light of the multiple serious injuries from the accident and other incidents that night. I hated needles, but there was no way I was going to allow my petty fear prevent my son from getting all that he needed. I gladly rolled up my sleeve and allowed the nurse to take my blood to give to my son.

About a half hour later, the doctor returned. He looked perplexed and apprehensive. I immediately thought Shelton had taken a turn for the worse and was distraught because his mother had not even arrived yet.

The doctor quickly reassured me that Shelton was going to be fine, but that they still needed blood for him. "I don't understand," I remembered tell him. "I gave you my blood."

"Yes, Mr. Calloway, you did. The problem is your blood type is not consistent with what Shelton needs. We need for his father or mother to come and give blood."

"His father? I am his father."

"I'm sorry, Mr. Calloway. You're not. Given your blood type and his, you are excluded as his father. The boy isn't your blood. I'm sorry."

I was crushed.

Thinking back to that day, I hung my head down and fought back the tears. In so many ways, that day marked the beginning of the end. I reached over to the passenger's seat and grabbed the bottle resting there. Guiding it to my lips, I took a deep drink. I would have finished off the liquor right then, except for the ringing of my phone.

"Hello?' I tried to enunciate the word as clearly as possible.

"Steven."

"Oh, hey, baby," I crooned to Monica, trying to take my mind off of Shelton. I knew it would be her without even looking at the number come up.

"Steven, do you love me?"

Monica's sudden and serious question snapped me to attention. I already had more problems than I could carry. The last thing I needed was Monica sweatin' me. "Look, Monica. I got a lot on my mind. What do you want?"

"I just want to know. Do you love me?" she insisted.

"Do I love you? Yeah, I love being with you." My goal was to answer her question and then quickly transition off the phone.

"No. Not do you love being with me. Do you love me? Do you want to be with me? Do you want to leave Crystal for me? I need to know."

I closed my eyes in frustration. Not now, I thought to myself. I don't need your insecurities. Not today. "We've talked about this before. It's not a good time for that. Matter fact, it's not a good time for us to talk about this at all. I got other bigger issues to deal with."

"You may think that now, but you won't after what I have to tell you."

"Come on, Monica. Didn't I say I'm not in a mood?"

"Well get in a mood, because Crystal, I now believe, knows about us, and you're going to have to make a choice."

Dumbfounded by her statement, I erupted in anger. "You no good stank ho. Why did you tell her? We had decided that it wasn't time yet."

She immediately became defensive. "There was no 'we' in it. *You* decided it wasn't time. And who the hell you callin' a ho?"

I forced my temper back into check. "Monica, I apologize. It's just that I told you from the very beginning that this wasn't a good time."

"Well, do you want to know what happened or not, Steven? I'm just trying to give you a heads up." I could imagine her sucking her teeth and rolling her eyes.

"Okay. Tell me. What happened? What happened?"

"When Crystal and I got ready to leave from the spa, a receptionist person referenced me as Mrs. Calloway and said something about having met my husband."

"Get the hell outta here. What did you do?" Images of Crystal going ballistic flashed before my eyes.

"I tried my best to play it off, but I don't know if it worked."

"Monica, wasn't there any way you could have played it off like she was talking to Crystal versus to you?" I didn't know how many times I had drilled it into Monica—deny everything.

"No. This wasn't the normal place that we both go to together. This was the spa where normally only you and I go. The normal place for Crystal and I was booked, so we came here."

"How stupid of you. You idiot." I couldn't believe Monica would be that thoughtless.

"Let me tell you one thing. How you talk to Crystal is your business, but I ain't tolerating you coming out your mouth like that towards me."

"Forget all that." I dismissed Monica's concern in light of the emergency we faced. "How did Crystal take it?"

"How did Crystal take it? You need to be asking me, how did I take it? I was embarrassed as hell."

"So, what did you do?"

"I told her you and I had bumped into each other in the mall while shopping. I told her I was on my way to Sweet Delights Spa and you thought it would be a nice gift to get her some gift certificates from there. There was a discount package if you bought a package of ten. And so, since it was cheaper to buy ten treatments versus seven, you bought the ten-pack and gave me two as a thank you gesture for having given you feedback on one of your new artists."

"What kind of convoluted BS is that?"

"It was the quickest thing I could think of."

While I didn't say it aloud, the words, "you dumb ho," kept reverberating in my mind. "Did she go for it?"

"Hell if I know? I just kept on sellin' it despite the fact that for a while you would have thought I was on the witness stand being cross-examined for having plotted to kill the President."

"Monica, I need to know, do you think she believed you?"

"Why don't you ask her? You seem to be so interested in what she thinks, how she feels. You want her number? You want me to do a three-way?"

"I'm not in a mood for your mouth. Didn't I tell you I got a lot on my plate?"

"Well, if you don't play your cards right and take heed to what I'm sharing with you so that you and I can be on the same page, Crystal's gonna have half of that plate."

Monica was right. I was playing a dangerous and potentially costly game. "I hear you. Is there anything else I need to know?"

"Yes. I done gave you enough time to get your act together and make a choice between her and me. And if you knew what's good for you and you have any sense, there really ain't no choice but me."

"Okay. I gotcha. I gotta get ready to go." Monica's overconfidence about what she had to offer was starting to annoy me.

"Don't leave."

"No. I gotta go."

"All right. Before you leave, I want you to know that I love you and I would do anything for you and for us."

"Okay."

"What do you mean, okay?"

"Okay," I repeated, but this time with an edge in my voice.

"I'll be damned if you're going to hear me say I love you and you don't say I love you back. Do you love me or do you not?"

"Monica, let it rest. Another time. Another time." I was becoming weary of her persistence, but I had had enough experiences with her to know that she wouldn't let the matter drop until she got what she wanted. "I promise you. We're going to do something very special together. Just let me handle what I got on my plate right now."

"Just one more thing...."

"Monica."

"Real quick. Have you spoken to Shelton about what we discussed?"

"Not yet, but I plan to."

"What are you waiting on?" fussed Monica. "Every moment counts. We don't know fully what he has told the FBI that can hurt you."

"I got it. I got it," my impatience was growing. "I know what the stakes are. I don't need for you to remind me."

"Steven, please understand. When you love someone, you don't want for them to hurt and you don't want for anybody to hurt them, because when the person you love hurts, then you hurt. You just want to protect the people you love. Do you understand what I'm saying, baby?"

"Yes. I understand."

"I love you and I will do whatever it takes to support you, because I love you."

"I recognize that."

"All right. Before you leave, I want to you hear you say I love you."

"Monica, I really, really, really care for you."

"Steven..."

"No. No more Steven. I gotta go. I'll call you back," I said

210

shaking my head.

"I love you, more than anybody. "

After I hung up the phone, my head hit the steering wheel. My whole life was crumbling before my very eyes. I had made a mess out of everything I touched. I needed to change, but I didn't have the power within me. As I sat there with my head down, my late mother's words unexpectedly came to me: "Call on Jesus," she had told me. "He came to save sinners."

At the time, I didn't even consider myself a sinner. I had it going on. I was living the American dream. Now, my life had become a nightmare. I could no longer lie to myself. I was lost, and I didn't know the way home.

"Jesus. Jesus. Help," I cried out. "I can't do this anymore. I'm sorry. Forgive me. Show me the way, and I'll follow You. You are the only One who has the forgiveness I need, because You are the One who died on the cross and rose from the dead. I need You. I can't do this on my own, and I don't want to." I sat there quietly feeling the anguish for all the destruction I had brought to my life and to the lives of others. I was broken and filled with sorrow for my sins, yet I felt an odd sense of hope deep within. Even with all that I faced and all the wrong that I had done, I somehow knew that now I could make it.

*   *   *

Crystal, as always, stepped out of the vehicle looking more like she was on her way to a fashion show than to an attorney's office. A recently hired private security guard helped push the few paparazzi back who knew about the meeting and its time.

I placed a couple of mints in my mouth in order to knock out the scent of the alcohol and started to slightly stumble my way across the busy intersection.

Just as I made it to the center line, I heard the first gunshot. It sounded like a diesel engine backfiring. By the second shot, I dove behind a car, reaching for my gun only to remember that I had left it in the car. I tried to gain my composure, even in my drunken stupor, so that I could make a mad dash down the busy street in the hopes that whoever was shooting at me would not pursue me as I ran against traffic.

Huffing and puffing and giving it everything I had, I raced up the street with such speed and grace that even an Olympic sprinter would have admired my technique and form. Several car lengths down the block, I noticed that people were screaming, "He's been shot. He's been shot." I immediately began searching my body for any bullet exit holes as I kept running at full speed.

As I ran around the corner and leaned up against a wall to catch my breath, I could feel my heart beating uncontrollably. There was not an immediate sign of blood, but that didn't mean that I wasn't shot. I started ripping clothes off my body. After closer inspection, I knew I was not wounded.

I then saw a lady running up the block screaming, "They shot him. They shot him."

I grabbed her by the arm, startling her, and yelled, "Who? Who?"

"They killed Killa C."

Falling to my knees, I called out, "Oh my God. Shelton's dead. Lord, why did You take him instead of me?"

CHAPTER TWENTY-TWO

Y ou don't have to be embarrassed. You can cry all you want. I understand. Shelton means the world to me, too," was my prayerful attempt to comfort the woman in a blood-stained blouse who had called 911 after having witnessed the up-close attempted killing of my nephew. Based upon the amount of blood lost, people thought Shelton was dead. News reporters and politicians were already spinning the shooting of "Killa C" as the next phase of an escalating hip-hop war among conflicting rappers. I suspected differently.

The shooting had occurred just before I had arrived back from the Caribbean. I saw that the new church staff member and congregant, Alexis Benson, had left me several messages on my cell phone saying that there was an urgent matter and for me to call her right away at Bernice Guitard Medical Center located off Paylor Drive. Since I had just gotten off the plane, I made the decision to postpone calling her for a while. I was enjoying reflecting on how great of a time I had had fellowshipping with the men during Anthony Thompson's wedding.

Before I dealt with all the worries and problems that people wanted for me to solve, I just wanted to have a few more minutes to think about how great it was to see so many men give their lives to Jesus Christ as Lord and Savior. They were men of all different backgrounds, educational levels and occupations, but what they all had in common was a level of understanding that no matter how good or bad life may be, it would be a whole lot better with God in it.

When I overheard the random conversation of two people in the airport discussing the shooting of a Black youth that had been on the news, I didn't even flinch. The killing and incarceration of young Black men on a daily basis was as dependable as the sun coming up and was occurring everywhere like the air. Every day, I prayed to God that He might use me in a way to bring about a change for our community and a whole generation of youth.

*　　*　　*

"Pastor Goodwell, you don't know me, but I've been attending your church lately, and I wanted you to know that I'm making sure that everyone on my staff provides the best possible hospital care that could ever be provided to Shelton Calloway," said a woman coming over to greet me as I entered the hospital and headed to the Intensive Care waiting area.

"Thank you and God Bless. That will mean a lot to the family," I sincerely replied and then gave her a hug. Before she left, though, I said, "Hold on one second. What is your name?"

"Mychele. Mychele Monroe."

"Well, Mychele Monroe, you make sure that you keeping coming back to visit at Mount Caramel. And when you see me, whether in church or outside, make sure that you come up and say hi if you got the time. I like to get to know the people who go to Mount Caramel."

"Yes, Pastor," she smiled in response.

"One more thing. Have you given your life to Christ? Because the most important thing during judgment day is going to be whether you came to Christ, not whether you came to church. There are a lot of church members at Mount Caramel and a lot of church people who are going straight to Hell. But what God wants is Christian disciples who know and live His Holy Word."

"Thank you for asking, Pastor. I am saved."

"Amen. I'm glad to hear that."

*   *   *

Standing in the waiting area, I didn't even have to turn around to know that the sniffling and crying that suddenly emerged from the hospital elevator was Crystal. I'd had too many good and bad memories of hearing that distinctive sound not to know that it was her.

Years ago I hadn't been supportive of her due to my lack of knowledge and understanding of the circumstances surrounding Shelton's birth, but when I heard the news that Shelton was the young Black man that the people in the airport were talking about, I immediately made a mad dash straight for the hospital. I was determined to be supportive to Crystal in ways that I had not been in the past. Shelton's gun shot wounds would give us a new shot at rekindling a friendship that I so dearly missed and cherished.

I took a deep breath to get all of my composure together, spun around and made my way to the woman whose tears and smile I had missed so much. Crystal was right where the sound of her tears had led me, but so was Steven.

Wrapping his arms around his wife to comfort her, Steven was where I wanted to be, but more importantly, Steven was where he was supposed to be. Despite all of my good intentions, I had to recognize a lesson that had been told to me a long time ago. Sometimes you just have to acknowledge certain things are not your season, and just because a person is a blessing, that doesn't mean that they're your blessing.

I didn't understand what God's total plan was for me, but I had grown enough in my faith to come to know that I needed to trust God. Faith for me was exactly that: F-A-I-T-H. For All I Trust Him and For All I Thank Him.

When I turned the corner, Steven and Crystal both looked up. Feeling awkward, I began to turn and walk away. I didn't want to be a burden in any way or to interfere with their relationship. We had all been through a lot.

To my surprise, however, the brother with whom I had not spoken in I don't know how long motioned for me to come over. I gingerly walked towards them, constantly praying to God over what to say or do, or if I should even be there. The number one thing that kept on going through my mind was, "Lord, let Thy will be done."

When I reached them, Steven, with tears in his eyes, gave me a big hug. It had been so long since we had even spoken let alone embraced. Even during the death of both our mother and our father, we had barely talked.

As I wrapped my arms around my brother, the irony hit me. I had been working so hard in the church and the community trying to be used by God to heal broken relationships yet not recognizing or appreciating that ministry first starts at home. There was healing that needed to occur between us, and the shooting of a child who belonged to neither one of us, but whom we both had wanted to claim at one time or another, had finally brought us together.

"Steven, I love you, and I'm here for you," I expressed with a deep felt sincerity that caused for me to choke up.

"Thank you. That means a lot," he replied as he squeezed me tighter.

After our emotional and healing embrace, Crystal, Steven and I held hands with one another in order to lift Shelton up in prayer.

"Our Father and Our God, we lift up this child into Your good and loving hands. Lord, we ask that You would heal him, because You are a healer. Touch his body, Lord. Be with the doctors, Father. Show them what to do. But even more important than healing his body, Lord, we pray that You would heal His soul. Father, we ask that you would give Shelton the opportunity to receive You and accept You as his Lord and Savior and to experience the grace and mercy and forgiveness that can only come through Jesus Christ. In Your holy name we pray, Amen."

"Have you spoken to the doctors?" I asked Steven.

"We did about 30 minutes ago," he explained as he held his wife's hand. "They're prepping him for surgery right now. They said the bullet had exited his body, but there was a lot of internal damage that they would have to repair."

"What kind of recovery are they looking at?"

"Well, they think he'll make a full recovery, but it's going to take some time, of course."

I nodded my head. "Some of my congregants work for the hospital. I'm going to see if I can get any additional updates. Do you need anything to eat or drink?"

"No. We're good."

As I turned to leave, Steven reached out and touched my arm. "DJ...," I could see the tears welling up in his eyes. "Thank you. I know we have a lot to resolve and a lot to forgive. This is just the beginning, and I really appreciate you being here."

I reached out and gave Steven a warm, brotherly hug. "I'm here for you," I reassured him.

*　　*　　*

As I made my way through the hospital in search of the head doctor on duty, a man called out from the end of the hall, "DJ, I mean, Reverend Calloway. Wait up."

When I saw my former college classmate approaching, a wide smile spread across my face. As we shook hands, I asked, "Do you work here now? I thought you were out West."

"I was for a while, but then the responsibility to take care of my aging parents brought me back."

"I know how that is. It can be taxing to take care of elderly parents, but it's important work."

"I heard about your nephew, Shelton. It's all over the news. I want to let you know that I will be overseeing his surgery. We'll begin in about 45 minutes."

"That's great," I said with relief knowing how talented of a doctor he was. "What can you tell me about his condition?"

"Well," he took a deep breath, "he's very fortunate in that the bullet missed a main artery. It ricocheted off his collar bone shattering it, but we'll be able to use pins to fit it back together."

"When will we be able to see him?"

"He'll be heavily sedated for several hours after the surgery and underneath twenty-four hour watch in the Intensive Care Unit for a few days."

"That sounds very serious."

"These are serious wounds, but I do expect that he'll make a full recovery."

"I'm glad to hear that."

"I'll do my part in the surgery; you do your part in prayer." As a fellow Christian, the doctor's understanding of the power and need for prayer reassured me that Shelton was in good hands.

"We've already been praying, and we'll continue to do so. God Bless you."

*　　*　　*

After speaking with the doctor, I felt God lift the blanket of heaviness that had been on me because of concern for Shelton. It was going to be a long night, so I decided to stop by the hospital cafeteria to purchase some snacks.

With all the rushing around, I had not had an opportunity to speak with my wife since leaving the Caribbean, even though I had left her several messages since my plane landed. I wasn't too worried in light of the spotty cell phone reception in the hospital. Now that the signal was strong, I tried dialing Vanessa's several cell phone numbers again, hoping to reach her. I even sent a text message to her on her BlackBerry, but she didn't respond. I checked my various phones for messages, but there was nothing waiting from my wife. That was odd. Even with her busy campaign schedule, Vanessa would normally check in periodically throughout the day. I decided to proceed to the cafeteria and try her again in a few minutes.

As I entered the hospital's main lobby in order to take the elevator to the basement, I saw De'Borah Harriston insisting that the volunteer who was manning the station for patient information respond to her questions.

"De'Borah, is everything all right?" I asked as I approached the desk.

"Pastor Goodwell, thank God. I've been trying to find out where Shelton is, but they said that they could only give out the information to family," she explained as she shot the volunteer a cool glance.

"I can take you to Crystal and Steven," I assured her. "Shelton will be in surgery soon."

De'Borah looked relieved, but as we took a few steps towards the elevator, she suddenly stopped and then covered her face with her hands.

"De'Borah?" I could tell she was crying. Softly I put my arm around her shoulder. "De'Borah, you're okay now," I tried to comfort her. "I'm sure it was very scary this afternoon, but you're safe now."

She let out a sob in response to my words. Not wanting her to become a public spectacle, I gently led her over to a corner of the general waiting area where several televisions were more likely to capture a passerby's attention rather than a crying woman.

For a few minutes, I just let De'Borah cry in my arms as I sat on the couch. I knew she had been in her office at the time of the shooting and figured she was upset about being so close to such violence. After a little while, she took a few deep breaths and dabbed at her eyes with the silk handkerchief she had taken from her purse.

"Thank you," she finally said as she let out a deep sigh.

"It's not a problem," I replied.

"I have some important information to share. I wanted to let you know that the District Attorney has decided not to indict Shelton. There isn't enough evidence to prosecute the case."

"De'Borah, that is great news," I exclaimed as I gave her a big hug. "Thank you for all that you've done for Shelton."

"You're welcome," she responded with a smile. "Now if you'll excuse me."

"Of course."

After De'Borah got up, I sat back on the couch, beaming. What a relief.

As I sat there, various local news programs were just beginning to come on. As expected, Shelton's shooting was the lead story on every network and their facts were essentially identical. After the 45 seconds of reporting concluded, I started to get up to try once again to reach my wife, when I heard her voice. Looking around, I quickly saw that she was actually on television, surrounded by a variety of community and church leaders, included Bishop Jackson from First Central Church, holding a press conference to express her dismay at the violence that she claimed hip-hop music was instigating throughout the state.

I stood there in disbelief that my wife was trying to politically capitalize on her nephew's tragedy. My anger was even further fueled when Bishop Jackson took the mic:

"During times like these, there's no better way to trust God than to trust your pastor," Bishop Jackson began. "We have leaders in this community who are wrongfully trying to divide us, but now is the time to come together. If we claim it, we can have it. We need to spread hope in this community. Everyone can go to Heaven as long as they believe in a god and believe that they're going there...."

"Damn false prophet." I couldn't believe it. I had labored so hard to diligently stay on the right path and faithfully follow God, and now my wife was joining forces with Bishop Jackson, the epitome of the watered-down, false teaching I stood against.

Shaking my head, I looked down at my phone as it buzzed showing that I had a new call coming in. I had been waiting for this phone call since I had arrived back in the States, so I enthusiastically answered the phone.

"Yo, Pastor, this is Prince Hall. I'm hitting you back like you told me to. Where do you want to meet?"

"I'm glad you called back, Prince. Let's meet in the same spot where we met before."

"You got it."

"Prince, since the last time we talked, have you learned anything on the streets about who might have shot Shelton?"

"A little something, here and there. Its definitely is not hood-related. Nobody really has a beef with the brother. I made extra sure that there wasn't anybody connected to me that was involved."

"The news media is blowing this into a hip-hop war. Whatever guy shot Shelton, we need to find out who he is quick in order that a lot of innocent lives don't get taken for a bunch of nonsense."

"I'm feeling you. By the way, it may not even be a guy. It may be a chick who shot Shelton."

"Get outta here. Do you think it was a groupie? A woman whom he dissed? Why would a woman be the shooter?"

"Look Pastor, I don't feel comfortable talking over the phone. Let's meet in person and build on our conversation from there."

"Cool. I will call once I get outta here."

*   *   *

As we waited for Shelton's lengthy surgery to conclude, Steven, Crystal and I watched a variety of sports on television as well as I caught up on the news I had missed while I was out of town. Most of the well-wishers had already left, except for a few of Shelton's former basketball teammates, several who witnessed the incident, and a handful of uniformed police officers who trickled in and out to collect statements.

During the fourth hour of the surgery, Crystal finally decided that she needed something to eat and offered to go past the cafeteria for Steven and me. As she took our orders, a new set of police officers entered the waiting area, except they were dressed in suits and wore their badges on their belts.

When they approached us, I asked, "Good evening, gentleman, can we interest you in something to drink or to eat? We're about to make a run for some food."

"Uh, no thanks," the taller one uttered shyly. "We're actually here to talk to a Ms. Crystal Calloway about a shooting."

Apparently overhearing their request, Crystal came over and introduced herself. "I'm Crystal Calloway."

"Mrs. Calloway, I'm detective Dunn and this is Detective Johnson. We would like to ask you a few questions about a shooting."

"Sure. It was extremely chaotic," she explained. "I came out of the car after Shelton, and before I knew it he was sprawled on the ground and bleeding. I think the bullets came from his left. I'm sorry I don't have any more information than that. It happened so fast."

"Actually, Mrs. Calloway, we're here for a different shooting. We'd like to ask you some questions about Evelyn James."

Crystal visibly tightened and then replied with an even tone devoid of emotion, "Not without my attorney present."

CHAPTER TWENTY-THREE

T he blind see and the lame walk; the lepers are cleansed and the deaf hear; the dead are raised up and the poor have the gospel preached to them. And blessed is he who is not offended because of Me.' " These are the words of Jesus Christ in the book of Matthew, chapter 11, verses 5-6. You may be seated."

As the congregation settled into their seats, I prepared to preach.

"This Sunday is an important day in the history of Mount Caramel, for this day, as a church community, we are going to recommit ourselves to Jesus Christ as Lord and Savior as well as look towards the future.

"Too many churches and ministers refuse to speak the truth to worldly power and remain silent on the troubling issues of our day. Instead of people in and out of the church being changed by God, people are instead choosing to change the Word of God to fit their sin and political agenda.

"People may not like it," I continued as I glanced over at the empty seat where my wife usually sat, "but I am going to stand here and tell you the truth. America is not nor has it ever been a Christian nation. America's religion is America. As a nation, America has falsely used Christianity and a nonexistent proclamation from God concerning its moral authority to proselytize the globe with its version of global capitalism and exploitation. The history of this country's economic and militaristic strength was built upon the slave labor and oppression of African-Americans for centuries. And don't you forget it.

"There are many good Christians in America, but that's a far jump to say that a nation with the legacy of oppression and discrimination that America has can call itself a Christian nation.

"And for all of you who don't know, I'm going to make it very clear. The Constitution is not the same thing as the Bible. The Founding Fathers were not prophets. And most importantly, the flag is not the cross. Despite the well-orchestrated campaign to try to confuse people into believing that these are the same thing and carry the same amount of weight, they do not.

"I am appalled at the number of preachers who are so busy trying to be treated like a king and building churches the size of miniature kingdoms that they don't spend time dealing with the issues that the One who is King of kings is concerned about.

"There are so many people walking around who are blind to sin. Paralyzed by despair. Lacking health care and healthy relationships. Dead to the truth about Jesus not only being a prophet but also Jesus being God. Dead to unemployment and spiritual decadence. Poor financially, educationally, emotionally and culturally.

"Just like there are drug dealers on street corners all throughout America pumping poison into people's bodies, there are also churches of all different sizes, with members of all different races and ethnicities, that are poisoning people's minds with false doctrines that will ultimately lead people straight to Hell.

"And to all my fellow pastors who truly believe in Jesus, we need to not only lead people to God, but when we see people who are earnestly seeking to have a relationship with God caught up and being led astray by false prophets who manipulate their pain and their desire for happiness and success, we need to expose to people the realities that there are wolves in sheep clothing who masquerade as men of God. We must expose the false prophets for what they are—false prophets.

"Everyone under the sound of my voice as well as anyone who professes to have a relationship with Jesus Christ as Lord and Savior or wants to needs to pray this: Jesus Christ, I accept You as Lord and Savior of my life. There is only one way to Heaven, and that is through You. All other ways lead to Hell. Lord, I acknowledge that Your Holy Word, the Bible, is true and that there are wolves in sheep clothing seeking to lead people away from You. Lord, I want to serve You and only You. I want to know You and not be led astray. I want a personal relationship with You. Reveal to me, Lord, who is of You and who is not as well as what is of You and what is not, so that the false prophets are exposed in my life. And give me the strength to break away from those who are false prophets. Convict my heart and mind as I study Your Holy Word and try to listen to Your Holy Spirit so that I may know, believe, and follow the truth of who You are. Amen.

"Now is the time to stand firm and stand tall. Are there any Christians out there willing to join me and other men and women of God and say, 'Enough is enough. We're going to take a stand against this new generation of false prophets by standing up and for God's Holy Word'?"

As the sermon continued, I explained the biblical text from Matthew's gospel. When the sermon ended, I was humbled to witness the move of God as people came forward to confess their faith in Jesus Christ as Lord and Savior. Yet as pleased as I was with that, there was another surprise I couldn't wait to share with the congregation.

"Your yesterdays don't have to define your tomorrow. God is still changing and redeeming people, but you have to trust God. We give praise to God for His awesome work in the lives of those who have come forward this morning. And in addition to our rejoicing on their behalf, I'd like to introduce you to another new member of our congregation who will be active with the youth ministry.

"You used to know him as Prince Murda. His birth name is Prince Hall, but if you were to ask him now, his focus is on the Prince of Peace, the Wonderful Counselor, and the Everlasting Father.

"Joshua Generation, stand up and let's give a warm welcome to our new brother in Christ, Prince Hall."

*   *   *

Entering into the Pastor's study, I removed my robe and relaxed in the leather chair exhausted yet renewed from preaching the Word of God. I then began going through my endless e-mail messages in the few minutes I had before I was scheduled to stop by the reception for those who had joined the church that day.

As I was getting to the end of my new messages, an anonymous instant message popped up on my screen:

"YOUR FATHER'S DEATH WAS NO ACCIDENT AND NEITHER WILL YOURS BE, IF YOU DON'T STOP WHAT YOU'RE PREACHING. YOU'VE BEEN WARNED."

CHAPTER TWENTY-FOUR

I've already made it into DJ's arms. It won't be much longer before I make it into his heart. But you and I need to have a heart-to-heart conversation ourselves. Why is Shelton's heart still beating?"

"You only told me to delay the ambulance whenever it came. I wasn't the shooter, so I don't know what happened."

"So who did you get to shoot Shelton?"

"You know I always have tricks up my sleeve."

"Well either way, he should have been killed. No excuses. It would have been just another unsolved hip-hop murder of a popular rapper. For all of our sakes, you better pray we kill him before he reveals everything he knows to DJ and the authorities."

"I sent DJ the message like you said."

"Good. The sermon that he preached today is going to cause us all different kinds of problems. But things are progressing on my end, too. He's named me his new Chief of Staff, so I know he doesn't suspect a thing."

"What's the plan?"

"DJ isn't the type of man to buckle under outside pressure. We'll have to do it from the inside. If he thought Vanessa was dangerous, then he hasn't seen nothin' yet. Just like Delilah with Samson, the best way to take down a man like that is to get him to love you enough so that he wants to believe even your lies and will trust you to the point of revealing his vulnerabilities. That's when we'll be able to seek revenge on him for all the chaos he's causing us. He's costing us a lot of money."

"I hope it works. With the elections not that far away, the stakes are getting higher and higher."

"It will. Trust me. You just keep working the political front. Jordan Clark is going to be our ace in the hole."

"I'm on it."

Without another word, De'Borah Harriston snapped shut the disposable cell phone and proceeded to the fellowship hall to join the other new members of the Mount Caramel Baptist Church.

Coming Soon!
Preachers' Row by S. James Guitard
The Sequel to Delilah's Revenge

The saga of Drama, Deception and Deliverance continues...
Don't miss it!

ABOUT THE AUTHOR

S. James Guitard is the nationally renowned author of three consecutive national best-selling books: *Chocolate Thoughts, Mocha Love,* and *Blessed Assurance.* His first book, *Chocolate Thoughts,* has consistently been rated one of the nation's best African-American books and has appeared on numerous bestseller lists. *Delilah's Revenge,* Mr. Guitard's highly-anticipated second novel, is a fast-paced, entertaining story full of twists and lessons learned that will have readers testifying and telling people how much they enjoyed it.

An exceptional public and motivational speaker, Mr. Guitard will be participating in book signings as well as radio/television interviews during his national book tour. In addition, Mr. Guitard is a featured consulting author of The Anointed Author Workshop Series, a comprehensive writing and publishing workshop for aspiring and contemporary Christian authors.

A native of New York who now resides in the Washington, DC area, Mr. Guitard has devoted his professional career to improving the quality of education for poor and minority children as a college instructor, administrator, school teacher, Capitol Hill lobbyist, as well as an education policy specialist.

L iterally Speaking Publishing House, one of America's fastest growing publishers of fiction and nonfiction hardcover as well as trade paperback books, is the publisher of several national bestsellers including *Blessed Assurance, Chocolate Thoughts, Mocha Love, Plum Crazzzy*, and *Checkmate*.

With its upcoming titles, *Illusions, Nowhere to Turn, Don't Mess with Me, Journey to the Light, Forbidden Fruit, Preachers' Row* and *Speak to My Heart*, LSPH is dramatically expanding its diverse mixture of first-time and veteran authors who uniquely capture life's joys and pains, fears and hopes, pitfalls and successes through refreshing characters, creative story lines and inspirational writing.

With its bold, refreshingly original and inspirational books, LSPH is becoming known throughout the nation as the home of "Writing that Speaks To You"—Writing that speaks to your experiences, dreams, desires, mind and most importantly, your heart. Welcome to the LSPH experience.

www.LiterallySpeaking.com

Additional Great Titles
from
Literally Speaking Publishing House
Available in Bookstores Nationwide

By S. James Guitard

A national bestseller, *Chocolate Thoughts* provides candid insight and uncompromising truth about how Black men truly feel about themselves, relationships, family, sex, marriage, work, careers, religion, love, money, racism, music, violence and sports. It uniquely captures the commonality of Black men irrespective of their socio-economic background or educational attainment.

Throughout *Chocolate Thoughts*, readers gain unbelievable access and understanding of the psychological, social, political and economic views that are often thought of but not often expressed by Black men to the general public. Being Black can definitely give the reader a connection to *Chocolate Thoughts*, but anyone irrespective of race or gender will find these writings to be thought-provoking, intimate, captivating, powerful, titillating and engaging.

ISBN: 1929642-37-7   Format: Paperback
ISBN13: 978-1-929642-37-3   Retail Price: $15.00

Additional Great Titles
from
Literally Speaking Publishing House
Available in Bookstores Nationwide

By S. James Guitard

A national bestseller, *Mocha Love* is a seductive, fast-paced, emotionally-moving and creative novel that reveals the challenges, obstacles and victories men and women face in life because of love, honesty, deceit and power. From sin to Savior, lust to Lord, world to Word, *Mocha Love* readers are exposed to a variety of heart-warming, romantic, masculine, intelligent, obsessive and strong men facing real-life temptations as they grapple with living a Heaven-bound life in a Hell-bent world.

Readers are able to probe the hidden, innermost thoughts and reflections of men as they make significant choices and decisions concerning marriage and infidelity, revenge and forgiveness, promiscuity and abstinence, corruption and power, faith and unbelief.

Mocha Love's originality is refreshingly honest and provocative. A wonderfully written novel, *Mocha Love* will touch your heart, your mind and your life.

ISBN: 1929642-33-4   Format: Paperback
ISBN13: 978-1-929642-33-5   Retail Price: $15.00

Additional Great Titles
from
Literally Speaking Publishing House
Available in Bookstores Nationwide

By S. James Guitard, Victoria Christopher Murray, Jacquelin Thomas, Patricia Haley, Maurice Gray and Terrance Johnson

With all of the chaos, confusion and uncertainty of life, we all need to know of the blessed assurances that God has for our lives. Fast-paced, witty, entertaining and inspirational, the writings in *Blessed Assurance* are modern day renditions of biblical stories. A national bestseller, *Blessed Assurance* is an enjoyable, empowering, engaging and encouraging example of the everlasting truth that God can move us from heartache to healing, burden to blessings, depression to deliverance, and from trials to triumphs.

In the short story, *The Best of Everything*, based on Hannah, you gain a better level of appreciation and thankfulness for what God has already done in your life, which will provide you with strength to endure in the midst of a crisis as well as give you patience as you await new blessings. *Lust and Lies*, based on Samson and Delilah, reminds us of the temptations of lust, the importance of honesty, the dangers of sin and the significance of repentance. *Traveling Mercies*, based on the parable of the Good Samaritan, teaches us not to place limitations on how and through whom God may send a blessing, as well as our responsibility to help people whom we often do not know.

Baby Blues, based on Abraham and Sarah, lets us better understand the importance of timing, patience and the consequences of operating in God's permissive will versus God's perfect will for our lives. *A Sprig of Hope*, based on Tamar, acknowledges that tragedy, sadness and betrayal are an unfortunate part of life, and yet ultimately there is healing, restoration and happiness if you place your trust in God. *Sword of the Lord*, based on Jephthah, confirms that your past can't define you if you give your future to God and that everyone at some time or another needs to forgive as well as receive forgiveness.

ISBN: 1929642-12-1   Format: Hardcover

ISBN-13: 978-1929642120   Retail Price: $19.95

An Excerpt from
BLESSED ASSURANCE: INSPIRATIONAL
SHORT STORIES FULL OF HOPE & STRENGTH
FOR LIFE'S JOURNEY
"Lust and Lies" by S. James Guitard
Based on Samson and Delilah

Night after night, the shapeliness of her legs and the voluptuous curves of her body kept calling me, so I kept calling her, the problem is, I've already been called—By GOD.

Tremendous, mind-boggling sex. Lustful rendezvous and misguided love have me lying in the bed, while lying to a woman who I know deep down doesn't really love me. Unfortunately, that hasn't stopped me from loving her, even if I can't trust her and my being with her conflicts with the Word of God that God has entrusted within me.

Sitting in the bed half-clothed, I watch her slowly parade across the bedroom floor wearing nothing more than a seductive smile. With a body like hers, it's hard to focus on her lips even when she's talking. Everything about the way she moves is constantly talking. When she says, "Look at me," I respond back with licking my lips and saying, "What do you think I'm doing?"

The rolling of her eyes and the placing of her hands on her hips are a sure 'nuff indication that she is not amused by my comment. "Look up here, Samson. I'm talking to you."

I honor her request even though my presence in her bed dishonors God.

An Excerpt from
Another Great Title
from
Literally Speaking Publishing House
Available in Bookstores Nationwide

By Monique J. Anderson

I always wonder why am I the one who continually attracts the misfit man, the dog, if you will. At this point in my life and with all that I have to give, one nagging question remains: Why am I not in a committed relationship with a man who has more than just words to offer, but is a man of his word as well as most importantly a man of the WORD? … Everything in me wants a man like my Father in heaven told me I should have. Loving. Dedicated. Sincere. Masculine. A real MAN.

A man like …

The night I met Mark I had on my favorite designer dress appropriately accessorized with a newly acquired purse and matching shoes. My revealing short skirt, while very attractive, made me feel a little self-conscious in church, but I got over it faster than the several pairs of eyes that kept looking at it… While fumbling in my purse for my make-up case, I heard a sound as though straight out of heaven….

"Excuse me, Miss," he said.

Tiptoeing like a graceful ballerina, I swirled around in slow motion. It was HIM. I hoped and prayed silently, "Please, Lord.

Please, Lord. Don't let me look as stupid as I feel."

With his hand outstretched, he introduced himself. "Hi. I'm Mark. Mark Hayes…."

ISBN: 1929642-07-5   Format: Paperback

ISBN-13: 978-1929642076   Retail Price: $14.00

Additional Great Titles
from
Literally Speaking Publishing House
Available in Bookstores Nationwide

CHECKMATE: THE GAMES MEN PLAY

By Mark D. Crutcher

The national bestseller, *Checkmate*, offers an entertaining, insightful, and empowering book for women to gain understanding of the dating process as well as the tricks and techniques men who are players vow never to reveal.

Checkmate provides uncut and uncensored access into the secret moves that men who are players use to win women's hearts, souls, minds and of course, their bodies. In a chess match, the objective is to place the opponent's king in an inescapable position on the game board. In the game that players play, the objective is to persuade women to maintain casual, uncommitted, sexual relationships with them. By the time women realize that a player's intentions are purely physical, it is too late. They are already addicted to the experiences they have shared and cannot or will not let go. Checkmate.

Checkmate: The Games Men Play will have you looking beyond your normal perception of reality and seeing the true meaning behind a man's actions and words.

ISBN: 1929642-50-4   Format: Hardcover
ISBN-13: 978-1929642502   Retail Price: $19.95